T0064691

The Corner

EDDY GUERRIER

authorHOUSE®

AuthorHouse™ LLC
1663 Liberty Drive
Bloomington, IN 47403
www.authorhouse.com
Phone: 1-800-839-8640

Published by AuthorHouse 06/25/2014

ISBN: 978-1-4969-2229-8 (sc)
ISBN: 978-1-4969-2228-1 (e)

Library of Congress Control Number: 2014911436

To my friend of many years, Mr. Jean Lacombe

DEVIL

From Wikipedia, the free encyclopedia

Depiction of the Devil as seen in the *Codex Gigas*.

The Devil (from Greek: διάβολος or *diábolos* = 'slanderer' or
'accuser')[1] is believed in many religions, myths and cultures

to be a supernatural entity that is the personification of evil and the enemy of God and humankind. The nature of the role varies greatly. It ranges from being an effective opposite force to the creator god at one extreme, where both are locked in an eons long holy war for human souls on what may seem even terms (to the point of dualistic ditheism/bitheism), to being just a comical figure of fun or even an abstract aspect of the individual human condition at the other.

Whilst mainstream Judaism contains no overt concept of a devil, Christianity and Islam have variously regarded the Devil as a rebellious fallen angel or demon that tempts humans to sin, if not commit evil deeds himself. In these religions – particularly during periods of division or external threat – the Devil has assumed more of a dualistic status commonly associated with heretics, infidels, and other unbelievers. As such, the Devil is seen as an allegory that represents a crisis of faith, individualism, free will, wisdom and enlightenment.

In mainstream Christianity, God and the Devil are usually portrayed as fighting over the souls of humans, with the Devil seeking to lure people away from God and into Hell. The Devil commands a force of evil spirits, commonly known as demons.[2] The Hebrew Bible (or Old Testament) describes the Adversary (Ha-satan) as an angel who instigates tests upon humankind.[3][4] Many other religions have a trickster or tempter figure that is similar to the Devil. Modern conceptions of the Devil include the concept that it symbolizes humans' own lower nature or sinfulness.

People often put the concept of the Devil to use in social and political conflicts, claiming that their opponents are influenced by the Devil or even willingly supporting the Devil. In addition, the Devil has also been used to explain why others hold beliefs that are considered to be false and ungodly.

THE STORY OF JONAS VICTOR

I Am Nobody

Jonas was on his usual corner, waiting for his customers to come by and get their substance for the day. Jonas was a small pusher who hated everybody, including himself. He never knew his father, his mother was a prostitute, and he lived in a poor neighborhood. He thought of himself as just a "nobody," living each day as it came and went. He used to be in high school, but he hung out with the wrong crowd and dropped out of school in the eleventh grade. When his former classmates were going to work or pursuing their studies, he was selling drugs on a street corner.

Today was his birthday. Jonas was twenty years old and had been working the corner since he was seventeen. Nobody told him happy birthday when he woke up that morning. He shared a small apartment with his mother in a project, but she was too high to even remember who she was, let alone that it was her son's birthday. Jonas did not have a girlfriend, and the people who called themselves his friends were actually his clients. His best days were always Halloween, Thanksgiving, and Christmas because, for some odd reason, a few of his customers found themselves obligated to give him a present, no matter how little it was. They were actually thanking him for helping them die quicker; how funny life can be! Hot or cold, he was always glued to his corner, knowingly selling death. He believed he was created by the Devil, and not once did it cross his mind that God existed for his kind.

No one would believe the things one could witness just by standing on a street corner; he had seen a lot, mostly the disintegration of his clients. At first, they usually came out of curiosity, but slowly and surely they became hooked on the merchandise and revealed the irreversibility of their situation. That was one of the reasons that he never touched his so-called medicine.

He had not arrived at that corner by accident or by his own choosing. They designated the place for him because of its convenience to where his supplier lived.

When he was in high school, the other students made life very hard for him. Since he suffered from asthma, he was not a good athlete, but gym class was a requirement, and he hated going. His physical looks were not that appealing. He grew to dislike his misfortune and the consequences that he had to endure because of his sickness and his frail looks.

The bullies used to walk by him making a wheezing sound and asking him if he was about to die. He always had to carry a vaporizer, which, to the delight of his classmates, he used frequently when he was short of breath. He had to take the medicine in order to regain normal respiration. For that they called him the pump man.

He grew up to practically hate them. One day he promised himself, he would get the last word. His mother did not like him either, especially when he started coughing endlessly when he had a crisis. Taking him to the doctor was another reason to complain. She said that he was costing her too much money, even though she always managed to be on welfare. As he got older, he matured slowly, and he wondered why on earth he had to be born. He was a loner with a sour face.

One day he met a guy in the neighborhood who seemed to give him the attention he'd longed for so many times. He thought that he was a sincere friend until he realized that he was grooming Jonas to sell drugs for him. At first he did not even know what those substances were. In orientation at school they always warned students against using drugs because they could either kill you or send you to jail for a long time. So far he had managed to avoid both those results, but there he was on that street corner, doing his job. When his feet were hurting him, he walked a few yards back and forth. He could not go too far from the corner because his customers did not have a schedule for coming to buy, and he had a quota to meet if he wanted to upgrade his commissions. His normal shift was about twelve hours every day, whether it was Sunday or Thursday or any other day. When he took a day off, he did not make any money. But his true motivation for being there was the hate he carried deep within his hearth against all the people who walked by as if they were better than him, those old schoolmates who were on the varsity team and only pretended that he was their best friend when their aching bodies were demanding their life substance.

Where he "graduated" from was one of the worse places in town. That street corner was a magnet for all races who needed to get high, buying from someone whose demeanor was as common as they came. Even the cops knew Jonah. He was such a small provider that they cruised by, just giving him a dirty look; they never apprehended him. They knew better: too small a fish. In order for him to be secure in the territory while doing his dirty job, he wore a small talisman made of two crossed axes with a two-fingered hand in the middle that all members of that gang of small dealers were given. Jonas never questioned the meaning of the medallion. He realized that anytime anybody wanted to pull him off his corner, by just flagging or showing it he was left alone. Now they were so used to him that he could go without that ID.

In school Jonas had always enjoyed the math and physics courses but was never too interested in the other subjects. He dreamed of becoming a big scientist, but instead the street corner became his laboratory. He had learned to detect deviant human creatures and their likes. Sometimes he was amazed to see them walk by as if they wished they were invisible against the walls; he knew very well what their problem was. They needed the stuff but did not want anybody to know that they were hooked. With them, the transactions had to be done quickly and discreetly. How discreet can you be if from time to time you came to him at that street corner? Anyone will finally get used to seeing you. Jason remembered one day he saw a young woman about his age just drop dead in front of him. The poor thing stayed too long in shock from deprivation, and when she finally had the money to sustain her habit, it was already too late; her entire system just shut down. And what about that guy who was suffering from post-traumatic stress? He never received one dime from the Veteran's Bureau, a problem of lost or mistaken identity, Jason heard. He was still fighting an endless war. He turned to some illegal activities in order to sustain himself. Instead of a token thank you for defending his country, he instead received a kick in the butt. He was bitter, and the drug was his only way out of his depression. What about the housewife who could no longer bear the sight of her husband and the children she'd produced for him? She was so polite, as if apologizing for sneaking to that street corner to get enough substance to help her to not go overboard or kill her husband. Jonas heard that she could not get out of the house because some family members came to spend a few vacation days with her husband, which finally pushed her to commit suicide. They were all different people with one thing in common: they were drug addicts.

Jonas never had a chance to experience the existence of God. He was surrounded by death and knew for sure that the Devil roamed among human beings at all times. To him, evil was the real thing. On his corner he inevitably saw a few prostitutes selling their flesh while their pimps cruised in their immaculate cars to make sure that their employees were at their designated posts in the open-air factory and meat market. He once saw a man pay one of the ladies of the street just to put his nose into her private parts while masturbating. At twenty, in spite of his controversial origins, Jason had never had any type of sexual relationship with either a man or a woman. Sex was part of all the things that degraded all human beings, and his place in life testified elegantly to his beliefs.

In fact, he was a virgin through no fault of his own, but the anger and disdain over his mother's activities did not help either. Probably he'd witnessed too young the use of sex as a means of financial relief. He guessed that for some, prostitution or other sordid means were a form of advancement too. He considered humans to be Nature's mistake; they had too many vices and imperfections. At night when he looked up at the sky, he always said to himself that somewhere up there must be an answer to all these questions.

One night he came home exhausted from standing and found his mother lost in her artificial world. The place smelled bad and needed some serious cleaning. They shared one bedroom. When a client was inside with her, Jason had to wait by the front door until they finished their business. One day he fall asleep there and nobody even bothered waking him up. They probably looked on him as the dog of the household. So that night he just went straight to the bathroom and took a shower. When he came out, he found her in the same position. Routinely, he checked on her and found a needle stuck in her right arm. She was deadly pale and dirty. When Jonas gave her a slight push, she fell right on the floor. The drugs had finally got the best of her; she was dead of an overdose. When they came and took the body away, Jonas had to think fast. He wondered how long it would take for the welfare people to find out his mother was dead. He decided to stay until that moment came.

Now he was truly all by himself, and nobody could care less about him. At last his mother was dead, after a life not worthy of evaluating. Probably wherever she went would be better than her life in the project. He did not even drop a tear for her and was glad that the municipality did not contact him for her funeral after he told them that there was nobody to notify. She was gone just like she came: a nobody. It took a few months before the welfare department was aware of her death and the money stopped coming in. Then he had to find a place to live. He was lucky to find a small studio nearby that was not above his means. He took what he needed from the apartment, threw the rest in the garbage, and gave the key to the superintendent. Jonas Victor was a complete unknown and looked like it.

Since his business was picking up, he went to his so-called main provider to tell him that he would like to move up in the system and make more money. The man looked at him and told him that he would take his request under consideration, but in the meantime he should go on doing what he was assigned to do on that street corner. While speaking to him, the man had looked at him like he was looking at a cockroach, which he probably was, and Jonas thought nothing of it because that was the way he felt. He went back to his street corner.

Across from where he usually stood was a small park where occasionally he saw children playing. It was shady and had a few iron benches. Sometimes when his feet were hurting him, he crossed over to rest his bones a bit. Jonas vaguely heard that the country was in a recession; his clientele was now more than ever mixed between regulars and newcomers looking for a substitute for the investments that went sour on the stock market. They were brave enough or desperate enough to venture personally to place their substance orders, making him wonder what they would do when they ran out of money. Aware of their despair, Jonas was told to raise the price of the stuff. He thought that things should be hard for them too. And the artificial escape that he was selling was good enough for them to forget for a brief moment the hardship they were enduring. He felt no pity for them and thought of them as bigger fools.

Contrary to what they showed on television, he was never molested, nor did anybody try to steal the merchandises he carried on him. The suppliers probably had their own way to make sure that he went on with his business without having to feel in danger at any moment. He looked so ordinary that nobody bothered to pay much attention to him. Sometimes his mind wondered far from that place, thinking of the amount of money and the risks that were taken by the organization so they could make these substances available and in his clients' reach. The drug user is always looking for a lost paradise that only exists in his mind. How stupid can that be?

Lately Jonas had been thinking of all the wrong reasons he dropped out of school. He was beginning to feel ashamed of himself and wondered what he could have accomplished had he continued with his studies. He could not get out of his mind the way that man, his supplier, had looked at him. He'd let some mindless classmates bully him out of school, or was that really their fault? He still at times opened his math and chemistry books.

With his mother's death, he felt an emptiness in his soul he'd never felt so deeply. Was it too late to find some type of redemption? The street corner had become his entire life. There had to be more than that. He did not think highly of himself, but he was no cockroach. All he needed was a *miracle*. The word resonated in his mind for quite a while, but life on the streets never stops. He was just a small drug pusher who did not know if he had a soul. If anyone would ever ask him what one word would describe him the best, he would say *loneliness*.

ILLUSORY HAPPINESS

One day he was standing at his usual corner when a marching band from the Salvation Army turned the corner, playing music and chanting along. The people in the group looked happy and proud of what they were doing. They did not need drugs to get high, they were already high on Jesus Christ and were letting people to know it while inviting them to come and rejoice in their faith and their salvation. Jonas wondered which of the two "drugs" were more potent, their faith or the substances he carried in his pockets. He would like to know the true definition of religion. He did not quite remember where he read that a man called Karl Marx wrote once that "religion was the opiate of the people," an "illusory happiness." Jonas was trying to establish the difference between what that man wrote and what he was doing on the street corner. This Marx man must have been a big intellectual who wrote big books, but how could he compare religion with drugs? It was beyond Jonas's understanding. He knew that his name or his occupation would never captivate the minds of any intellectuals because he was a nobody. However, the stuff he was selling did attract the noses and veins of many who would not give him a second of their attention.

Jonas always carried a sourness in his stomach against most humans. No one ever looked at him with compassionate eyes. Even when they came to buy their stuff they could not look him in the eye. He was not what interested them, only the provider of the illusion or euphoria that they were seeking. Maybe he was a rat coming from sewage. Even though he knew that he had a brain—he could still remember certain classmates copying his math and chemistry homework. They could not understand anything about the design of numbers, the regulated reality of the universe, or the movements of chemical elements that surrounded everything. But he could, and he enjoyed the fact that his mind was predisposed toward such things. He knew that he was not dumb or stupid, but he never had a chance to free himself from the grip of his birth, or so he thought.

He was disgusted with those people. He remembered a woman coming to buy drugs from him who was accompanied by a child no older than eight. When an innocent creature was already exposed to that sort of behavior, what could you expect from that child once he grows up? Jason was lucky that he was so uncomfortable with his mother that he never wanted to know or to have anything to do with her except share that one-bedroom, where he'd always slept on a mattress as long as he could remember. Probably he was born with the Devil print somewhere on his back.

One day a guy was so desperate that he came asking him if Jason could sell him some stuff on credit and became very agitated when Jonas said that he could not. He was rather big, so Jonas stepped away from him, but he menacingly walked toward him. In a moment two guys came out of nowhere and stuck a knife in the man's belly; he died just a few feet away from Jason. Not even the police asked him any questions. That day he realized that in spite of all appearances he was under constant surveillance.

Jonas looked up at the blue sky, wondering what exactly was up there. Lately he had been feeling uncomfortable in his own skin. He had strange dreams of vague, ghostly people talking to him in a language that he could not understand. One night he saw them in fist fight, and he was apparently the reason for their dispute. He woke up that morning feeling very cold and wet; a pipe by his bed had a leak he had to tell the super about. After taking a quick shower he started his routine, which he knew for sure would be just like any other day. He stopped by a delicatessen to grab a good sandwich and a hot coffee. Then he walked slowly to his vending point since he had already seen the supplier the night before. Nothing was abnormal on the corner. After a few minutes the customers started to come. Some of them smelled rather bad, which told Jonas that they had not even bothered to wash for days.

Sometimes he wondered where they got the money to sustain their habits since they did not look that dangerous or that attractive to him. He knew that money did not grow on trees. While his mind went back to that idea of "illusory happiness," he saw an old man sitting on the bench where he used to go and rest his feet. The man was looking straight at him. At first he did not pay much attention to him. He thought that he could be one of these old addicts whose bodies were boiled dry by the drugs they'd used most of their lives, but there was something different about that old man.

Being a creature of lonely habits, Jonas did not pay much attention to the old man and went about his business. Late that afternoon, when he was about to close "business," as he used to say to himself, the old man was still there, as if he'd never moved. That night, again, Jonas had the same dreams. He thought that it was probably something he had eaten, since he was no drug user. Nonetheless, those types of dreams did not fit his personality. Like any human being, he dreamed at night, but he always forgot what he dreamed once he woke up. But these dreams were persistent, like a scratched CD—endless.

Every single day the old man was at the same place, watching him, and every single night Jonas had been having the same dreams. He felt a sense of anticipation of things to come but could not put it into words.

THE STEPS TOWARD THE OLD MAN

The presence of that old man from across the street started to have an effect on him for some reason, as if he were being watched. From a distance he stole a glance at the old man. He was of medium height and skinny, but even though he was of an advanced age, it was impossible to guess how old he was. His face was calm and serene, and he seemed to be wearing the same clothes since he'd first seen him. Jonas was busier than usual lately, and he was tired of seeing those stupid people coming to buy something that would only destroy them. He wished that they would stop coming, and then he would be forced to look for something else to do. The drugs that he was selling started to have a psychological effect on him. Every time a client came he felt a dart pinching his heart. He questioned this, since he did not market the stuff and did not force anyone to come to him. Why did he have the feeling that he was the one destroying them? Why this guilt?

In spite of all that, something was impeding him from crossing the street to get closer and have a good look at that old man. He was being held back for no apparent reason. It seemed the old man could not harm a fly, let alone someone like him who knew the ropes of this street. So Jonas went on doing his business and tried to forget the man right across the street.

That night his dreams were more intense and somewhat violent. Something was trying to harm him. A strange creature came to his defense but not quickly enough to avoid him being wounded. Jonas felt the pain. It woke him in the middle of the night. He ran to the toilet and vomited everything that he'd eaten that evening. What on earth was going wrong with him, he wondered. The following day Jonas decided to cross that street when he saw the old man at the same place; one might even think that he'd never left. He went and sat by the old man and looked at his profile. He knew that the man was aware of his presence beside him but did not turn to look at him.

- You finally came, Jonas.
- How do you know my name?
- It is my business to know everything. What took you so long?
- I've been watching you for quite a while.
- I know, but you were hesitant to come. Why?
- Something was holding me back.
- Nonetheless, you came—that's what is important.
- Can I offer you something?

15

- Yes, your undivided attention.
- You got it.
- You look terrible, Jonas. You have not been sleeping well lately.
- What is your name?
- You can call me Old Man, just like you've done since the first time you saw me. And no, you cannot offer me anything. On the contrary, I can offer you a lot.
- Such as?
- Your true self.
- I've never met you before.
- But I have known you all your life. Let me ask you a question. Do you believe in God?
- God is what you make of it, and based on my birth and my life, I don't think that such entity exists.
- You cannot be more wrong.
- Then I must have been cursed from the first second I was conceived in a prostitute's womb.
- There is a lot of bitterness inside you, but tell me— why did you choose this trade to appease your fellow men?
- I believe that the trade chose me, since I'm a nobody.
- Is that the reason why you left school, even though you are good at science?
- You do know a lot about me. What do you want from me?
- First, I want you to find your true self, because you do have a lot to do.

- By selling drugs on a street corner?
- No! But since we are on the subject, tell me what you really think of mankind.
- A mistake of creation.
- Why?
- Since you seem to know so much, you must see that all we do in this life is accumulate unfulfilled dreams that cause us to lose ourselves in everything that affects our mere existence, be it too much work, too much pleasure, drink, drugs, and the like, until one day we get sick or get in an accident and finally die.
- So if I understand you correctly, everything is trivial but *death?*
- You can say that. Look at them, putting this stuff in their bodies, knowing that it will not come to any good, but they do it anyway.
- But you never told them to stop. On the contrary, you seemed to enjoy their degradation.
- They never did care much about me, so why should I about them?
- Ho! I have a great deal of work to do with you in order to prepare you of what is expected of you. You will start by listening and asking questions when needed. Selling drugs is over for you, or you will be so tormented at night that you will *beg* to see me again.

Jonas heard a car making a loud sound. When he turned to look out of curiosity, he saw nothing. By the time he returned his attention to the old man, he was gone, as if he'd just vanished.

Jonas did not have any religious affiliation and never thought of having one. The recent events in his somewhat banal life made him think of the urge that some people had to pray to God or go to a church. Those people looked like regular folks trying to live their own lives. What type of closure did they find in sitting and talking to an entity they could not see and that never talked back to them? Granted, he was still a young man, but life had not been good to him. He truly considered himself a burden to humankind because he carried to others one of the worse damnations that could happen to any human being: *drug addiction*. Jonas knew the difference between good and bad. Nobody had to teach him that, but he carried a grudge against all the people who bullied him and those who made his deceased mother what she was, a common prostitute. That sour-acid effect never left his thoughts or his stomach. Since he'd always loved mathematics and science in general, if he were to define himself, he would have picked the number zero to the infinite power. Now he had to deal with the obsession of an old man who excelled in making him guess answers for which he never raised any questions. His disappearing act did not help either. Were the drugs in his pockets found a way to get to his brain? That would be a rational explanation, probably.

When his mother died and was buried, he threw out most of her possessions. They were worthless to him. However, he kept two things he found in her belongings: a picture of him when he was a toddler sitting on her lap and a Bible. She was not a bad-looking woman, but she'd wasted her life nonetheless. Maybe her physical attire played a role in her downfall. Who knew?

WHY THOSE DREAMS?

Jonas was determined not to have any of those funny dreams that night. He bought a good bottle of blended scotch and had a few shots before he lay down to rest his bones. For some unknown reason he clutched the Bible in his left hand. Like they say, you never know. Maybe this would help keep all the demons away from him. But they made matters even worse. That night he saw that he was in a deserted land, all alone, and the sun was scorching his skin. At a far distance he could see something that resembled an oasis, but the faster he walked, the farther away the point got. Behind him a hyena-type animal was looking at him, keeping a safe distance. Apparently it was waiting for him to get weaker or die so he could become his next meal. Jonas was very afraid of the beast. He tried to scare him away, but the animal made a gesture with its muzzle that could be interpreted as a mock smile. With all the strength he had left, he tried to reach the oasis.

At one point when he turned to locate the beast, he saw by its side a beautiful naked woman with an apple in her right hand and a bottle of water in her left hand. Jonas could feel the thirst scorching his throat, but all he wanted was to get to the water hole surrounded with palm trees. Only in pornographic pictures had he ever seen nudity in his life, but the lady was also teasing him with her tongue, which appeared longer than usual. Now the beast was getting restless, and Jonas felt that it was on the verge of making its move to attack him. He was aware that his situation was going from bad to worse. All of a sudden, out of the sky came a big white bird that practically engulfed the woman and the beast. Afterward the bird cleared a path for him that led him directly to the oasis. The place was cool and relaxing. Out of the trees came out the old man he used to see right across from his street corner. He told him:

-    Welcome home, my son.

Jonas practically collapsed in his arms, crying like a baby. He felt tranquility and comfort. The old man gave him water to drink, food to eat, and bathed him. When he finished he told him to rest a bit because he had a long road ahead of him. Jonas wanted to know exactly where he was going, but the old man only told him that his heart would show him the *way*.

The last word resonated in his mind, until he woke up with a terrible headache. One could say, in a strange way, that the word *way* made Jonas shiver with fear of an unknown outcome. The toilet seat was cold when he sat on it, but it was time to think about the many questions he had in his head. He really had a bone pick up with that old man once he saw him again. He'd never once spent time to think if there was something beyond death, never thought of Heaven and Hell—those words were not included in his way of thinking. He was just a *nobody*. And now apparently he was at a significant milestone in his "senseless" life, he thought, not knowing what was truly happening to him. It was impossible that the mere sight of an old man could trigger so many abnormalities in his day-to-day living. He had to put a stop to it.

The first thing he did that morning was go see his supplier in order to give him back the rest of the stuff he hadn't sold; he put his account in order with him and told him that he had a few personal things to handle. Therefore he would not be available for a few days. The man looked at him the usual way and just told him that whatever he had to do was okay with him, as long as he kept his mouth shut if he cared for his life.

Having done this, Jonas went to where he used to see the old man. Sure enough, he was already there.

- How are you, my son?
- First of all, I am not your son, and most of all, who are you?
- Are you asking me this because you have not been sleeping well lately?
- Just tell me who you are.
- I am just a messenger.
- Then what is your message?

- It is time for you to start your journey.
- What are you talking about?
- The journey to your mission. Go back to your small studio with me so you can take the Bible your mother left you and that picture you've looking at. Then you will have to follow me.
- Just like that?
- Yes, just like that.

Jonas could have done many things. He could have laughed, walked away, stayed seated, or completely ignored what that stranger asked him to do. However, any human being has a sixth sense, and his told him to do exactly what that old man told him to do, although Jonas was very confused by his own reaction. In a glimpse of a moment, Jonas saw that so far his life really had no meaning whatsoever. Therefore, what did he really have to lose by finding out what this old man was all about?

Jonas collected exactly what was asked of him from his room and followed the old man. When they stepped out, a car with a chauffeur was waiting for them. He did not even ask where they were going. They drove out of the city. After about what he would say was a one-hour drive, they drove into a wooded area where he saw a beautiful cottage by a small river. The area was very peaceful. He could only hear the birds and a small breeze in the middle of the trees. It was very peaceful and restful. They got out of the car and sat on a porch. It was only then that the old man started talking to him.

- You've had a rough and empty life so far, Jonas.
- How do you know my name?
- I thought you told me…
- What is yours?
- Old Man is good enough.
- You seem to know everything.
- Yes.
- What is next?
- Don't be in such a hurry.

The cottage was very humble inside, with all the required necessities and no more. The old man showed him a bedroom that was to be his. On the bed were a white robe and a few toilet utensils. Jonas undressed and put the robe on. When he stepped back on the porch, he saw the old man was dressed just like he was.

- Are you some type of Muslim, or do you belong to a cult?
- Because of the robe? No! It's just more relaxing and neutral.
- Are you preparing me for some type of trip or initiation?
- It is good that your mind is starting to function in the right direction. If I were for starters to ask you to show me God, what would you say?
- Nothing. I don't even know if he really exists.
- He does, but what would be your answer?

- For me, if he truly exists, God is a being with a lot of discrimination. Some people He likes and others He does not give a damn about. I'm sure He created everything, including poverty and misery.
- I could start by telling you the contrary, but since you seem to trust me somewhat, I would prefer that you spend time in reading the Bible. Keep in mind that this holy book was written to be told, not read. Furthermore, you have to read three ways: like a story book, like a spiritual book, and, finally, like a mystical book.
- I'm not an avid reader.
- Try anyway. I reassure you that I don't intend to give you bible lessons, like you probably have heard religious pastors and priests do. However, I want you to start with what is common to many people from your side of the world—the real *truth*. If you were a Muslim, you would have read the Koran already. Remember, you have all the time you will need before the next step.
- So it *is* some type of initiation that you are working on me?
- Keep an open mind—it will be all for the best.

Jonas kept an open mind. He needed a change of scenery and some rest. He took his time reading the Bible; it was the first time he was reading it. He was amazed to find the book captivating. He was surprised to see that violence and sexually bizarre situations were in the Old Testament. As for the New Testament, everybody had heard of Jesus Christ, but he did not know how revealing this reading would be regarding his mission. Seldom did Jonas see the old man, but he had enough to eat and was never disturbed by a person or any strange noise. It was as if he were all alone on Earth with this book. He could not say exactly how long he spent just reading, but one thing was certain; he felt at peace and in no hurry to leave this place.

One day he was seated on the porch when out of nowhere came the old man. There was only one way to say it. He looked rejuvenated.

- How have you been lately, Jonas?
- Reading and feeling well.
- Good. In two sentences, tell me about the Bible.
- The Old Testament is the story of a bunch of people looking for a place to stay. And the New Testament is the story of a hippie-like guy and his friends having some hard times with the Romans.
- Very graphically put.
- You told me two sentences.
- Yes. Was it good reading? Tell me what words of wisdom you took out of reading this book.
- First, it was good reading, and I got two words of wisdom out of all this. They are *perseverance* and *faith.*
- Good! I must say that I am surprised. You will need these words on your journey.
- What if I had told you something else?

- All words have a meaning that can be put to use, as long as you respect the context from which you took the words.
- You never cease to amaze me.
- Likewise Jonas, likewise. I know you like science, especially math and physics, correct?
- Yes I should have stayed in school to become a great scientist, because I can relate to these things. Don't ask me why, because I don't know.
- You will know why.
- Apparently there is no past, present, and future for you, from the way you carry yourself and speak.
- Jonas, don't waste your time on pointless speculation. Start thinking like a circle. It will give you a better understanding of what you are about to learn and do. Be prepared. Everything has a meaning and a reason, but everything is also limited by the extent of our thinking and on how we handle our moment of enlightenment. Remember that. By the way, the hippy-like guy you mentioned—I would rather you call him by his name: Jesus Christ.

Somehow between His name and his hippy-like version of that peace-and-love era, many things were lost in his reconciliation, such as all the drug use, the insatiable sex, the carefree living, and all the unfortunate acts that occurred during that time.

The old man did not raise his voice, but something in his tone of voice commanded respect. For the first time since he met him, Jonas realized that this man, regardless of his appearance or his age, could also be dangerous, especially when he added:

-    You will have to unite the weak and the strong.

A sixth sense indicated to Jonas that the situation he was embarked on was real, and along the way he would find the true meaning of the life that he thought was senseless. He was beginning to sense that this old man truly knew his real calling, whatever it would be. All he had to do was to follow his teachings. He was certain that something good would come out of this, giving a new leaf to his existence, a *mission*. Jonas knew that all he had to offer were his youth and his curiosity to learn a notion that eluded his way of thinking but attracted his needs to pursue a meaningful existence. In a way, he felt that the old man already knew that urge was buried deep inside himself. In his short life he'd experienced a great deal of loneliness. However, while reading the Bible he felt a sense of belonging and believed that what human beings called God had a strange way of establishing the necessary mystical connection between Him and those who were wise enough to follow His precepts. He noticed how violent the Old Testament was in comparison to the New Testament. He also realized that physical suffering did not necessarily affect your mind and your soul. He saw the different aspects of love and self-denial for the benefit of others. He sincerely thought that Jesus Christ did not have to let himself be so humiliated for the love and salvation of others, since the world had not changed that much since the time of his crucifixion. Apparently people better understood the wrath of the God portrayed in the Old Testament rather than the tender approach of Jesus. However, he was certain that the old man would help him establish the correlation and the necessity of both aspects. He only had to wait.

Jonas Victor did not have to wait long. After his lengthy reading of the Bible, hc had several spiritual conversation with the old man on several subjects, from humans on earth to the universe as a whole. His teaching was never about religion but mainly about God and the holy gift hidden in mathematics. He also spoke of the different levels of human capacity to comprehend elements of their own being. The old man never tried to give a definition of God; better yet, what he explained was so simple that it made Jonas thinks even more. During all his considerations, he always said to Jonas that God was everywhere and in everything. And this was sufficient food for anyone's thoughts.

Late one evening he came to the cottage and told Jonas that he was going on a learning voyage. He added that he did not need to take anything along with him. They sat down on the porch, and the old man told him to join hands with him and to relax. As long as he lived, Jonas would never forget what was about to happen to him. He felt that he was losing consciousness and being thrown in a vortex full of stars and mathematical symbols, many he did not recognize. However, he had enough rationality to understand that he was actually time traveling toward another universe.

PAMPUYO

With baited breath he saw himself land on a strange planet called Pampuyo, with two suns or two moons, he could not say. One was orange and the other blue, and both were turning the atmosphere into some type of vapory wonderland. The place was inhabited by people of different races, some of which he did not recognize, but all were wearing the same white robe the old man had given to him. There was no welcoming committee, but somehow he felt that there was no need. Instead of walking, everybody was floating from one point to another. Several groups were gathered under huge trees, looking at what seemed to be teachers. But Jonas did not actually hear any sound except for a subtle music that enclosed the entire atmosphere. He was able to understand what the teachers were explaining. He finally realized that they were mind communicating, and this type of learning process went much faster, like simple osmosis.

Jonas could not say actually how much time he spent learning different subjects, including mathematics and sciences, especially physics. Everything was done mainly through mind-concept communication. However, many times he felt an invisible presence looking over them. The feeling was always peaceful and engaging. From the attitude of the students, he realized that he was not the only one who felt this manifestation; the feeling was the same. During all this time the old man was nowhere to be seen. But Jonas knew he did not get there by his own means. Another strange thing he noticed was that nobody slept, and there were no clocks or bells indicating the passing of time. However, there were times when the teachers were not visible and they all intermingled, having light conversations but few questions, all through mind communication.

One day they floated to another place, where the people or creatures were not like them; they were ugly and evil. When they saw Jonas and his companions, they tried to avoid looking at them directly and tried to keep their distance, as if they were ashamed of something. He saw that these groups also had the same teachers, but it was obvious that their learning was not as smooth as for the first group to which he belonged. They were stubborn and reluctant, and the presence he previously felt did not convey the same sense of togetherness. On the contrary, the presence was at times even menacing and intimidating until they bowed to his demands through much torment and confusion. However, the High Spirit always prevailed, and once the creatures accepted the teaching, the presence became soothing and comforting, like a father toward his once-reluctant kids.

Jonas did not see in this land any burning places or any unbearable climates. It was a vast open-air school of different levels and methods of teaching. Afterward Jonas saw himself back to the original place, where his teaching continued. And the old man was nowhere to be seen. He wondered what had happened to him. Was he on another assignment now he'd dropped him where he was? One thing was certain for Jonas: whatever time he had spent so far in this place, he'd learned a great deal. His mind had reached a level of awareness that no school could have given him. Somehow he knew that his stay was coming to an end. He was not the only one leaving while others were arriving. The same vacuum that took him in that place picked him up, and he saw himself on the bench on that street corner. Surprisingly, the old man was by his side. But something in him was different; he felt it more than he knew it.

- How long was I gone?
- Three years in their time, about three minutes in your time.
- I am not following you. How did we get on this bench? The last time I was with you was in the cottage, on the porch.
- You got here for the same reasons you were sent there. Time is irrelevant. What it's important is what you have learned. Have you ever heard of Albert Einstein?
- The man who made the atom bomb.

- He never made any bomb. Just because I show you how to use a fork and a knife to eat, if you decide later on to kill someone with those tools, does that make me the inventor of a killing machine? Certainly not. The knowledge that you have just received will allow you to better understand mankind within our universe and will also help you in your mission, which is to help your fellow man. You stood on that corner to push drugs. Now your time has come to push the good Word of our God.

- Why me?

- Why not you? He saw in you all the capabilities you need to confront what you are about to do.

- But me doing this? Who will believe me, and would I change the world?

- If someone had to consider each drop of water separately, would he ever have a full glass to drink? Don't worry about the ways God fills the glass. Just contribute to its fulfillment.

- Where do I start? When do I start? What will I say? Or will I go on telling people that I've been reborn?

- First, you did not die, so let us not dwell on that expression. All I can tell you is to follow your inner self and never forget that God is great.

THE BEGINNING

The old man left the same way he came, without adding another word. Jonas knew that his life had changed forever. Resolute to make good of what he had learned, he stood up. He planned to go back to his small apartment wearing the same clothes that he had on when he went to the cottage with his Bible in his hand. That's when he felt the cold metallic nose of a firearm on his back. Then he was pushed into a car that sped off rapidly. He knew he was in some kind of trouble. They took him in a deserted alley, where he met with his supplier.

- So you have decided just like that to leave this job?
- This was not a job.
- It was for me. I don't like people making a fool out of me.
- I have decided to stop working for you.
- And what will you do?
- I will be pushing the word of God.
- Don't make me laugh!

- I'm quite serious.
- That is why it's been reported to me lately that you spend your time sitting on a bench right across from your street corner, doing nothing or watching our activities to report to some other gang?
- I've been sitting on the bench having a serious conversation with an old man.
- Stop joking. Nobody saw you with anybody. All they told me was that they saw you talking to yourself. Have you been using the stuff I gave you to sell? Your account is correct, not a penny short.
- I never used the stuff.
- Nobody leaves me like this.

Jonas got one of the worst beatings of his life. They hit him so hard that after a while he lost consciousness. When he regained his bearings, he stood up and went to his studio to tend to his wounds. While he was sitting on his small bed, he thought it very strange that nobody saw him talking to that old man.

But after his recent experiences, this thought did not disturb him. So many things had happened to him. One thing was certain; he had to visit a few churches because his new-found faith and his recent experience meant that he needed more knowledge in order to accomplish his mission. His goal was simple. He would go to churches with different religious practices and explain as clearly as he could what had happened to him, from the old man to Pampuyo. After that he would decide what he needed in order to start his pilgrimage.

For Jonas, it was a simple task. The people he was approaching were responsible for guiding their fellow men toward the right path for their salvation to bring them closer to God. He went to a few of them. Although they received him with kindness most of the time, he could see that they thought that he was somewhat crazy, but not in a dangerous way. That's probably why they did not report him to the police. Surely if he were to part the sea like they said Moses did, he would have belonged to the rare individuals touched by God, but he knew better.

One day while eating alone, he reflected on the human nature. We like extravaganzas, things that impress us and make us feel small and vulnerable. We don't know how many qualities God instilled in us, but one of the most powerful is *to love one another*.

FINDING THE LIGHT

Jonas overcame some of his misconceptions. Not all who were entitled to guide the others to the true word of God knew where to begin themselves. They limited themselves to the literal reading of the Bible, without making the intellectual effort to go beyond the words, the regular daily and weekend prayers, yelling God is great with no other effort on their part. Jonas tirelessly spent a lot of time in libraries in order to read about of the post–Jesus Christ era through the involvement of the Roman Empire in Catholicism. The transformation of Christ's teaching into the grandiosity of Rome and beyond baffled him. If only he could find the old man, he could confide in him, but obviously his mission was somewhere else. Presumably he felt that Jonas could find his way all by himself. He reminded himself of his stay in Pampuyo, a place that he came to understand but that he could not explain to anybody else. Nonetheless, the changes that occurred in him were very real, and now he could feel that he was not alone.

One day while surfing the Web in the library, he found an article on the Salesians of Don Bosco, which at great length said that the Salesian priest was ordained to teach and guide youth while seeking to facilitate in a Christian way their needs for love and understanding while also providing them with good scholastics.

This reading struck a chord in Jonas's mind. However, he had heard so many bad things about religion lately and the sins that had been committed that he was somewhat hesitant to seek their teaching. He needed some time to think.

One day he went to a Catholic church and sat down, looking at the cross on top of the altar. And he said to himself, So much suffering, and for what?

He was begging to understand, because as he saw it, the world had not gotten better since that big sacrifice. He did not notice when an old priest came and sat by him since he was still staring at the cross. The priest told him:

- What you are looking at is a representation of His Passion, not an answering device. If you want to confess, I am here to guide you.

Jonas turned and looked at the priest, whose face was ageless. One could feel that he had already found solace and redemption.

- I'm not here to confess my sins. I am only starting to understand the religious definition of sin. I'm looking for a better way for me get closer to what I have learned about true self-denial in order to serve the most as is humanly possible.

- Realizing what you have done is already a step in the right direction.

- I think that I want to become a Salesian.

- Just like that you came to that decision?

- No, I've been searching for a while. I've been in and out of many churches and heard many pastors before I finally made that decision.

- You know that there are many ways to serve.

- Yes, I know, but for me there cannot be any other way.

- The learning is long and tedious.

- I have all the time in the world.

- Do you have any family?

- No.

- What studies did you do?

- Many and little, but if I were to tell you just what I experienced before, you would think that my head is not straight, that the only reason that I'm not locked up some place is only because I cannot do any harm to anyone.

- Would you be willing to tell me your story if I promise not to mock you?

- I don't trust many of your kind either. You've been molesting children and projecting a different picture from what you were supposed to.

- Indeed we committed a lot of mistakes and sins, but who are you to judge those who did these crimes? Do you know what amounted to their punishments?

You made a choice after certain research you did all by yourself. But becoming a priest, especially the one you look forward to becoming, requires a lot of studies and self-denial. Above all, I would like to hear your story. Let me invite you to break bread, and then you will have plenty of time to talk.

- Okay.
- By the way, my name is Father Henry.
- And mine is Jonas.

Father Henry was a shabby man with broad shoulders. Later he explained to Jonas how he loved growing plants. He told Jonas that he was from another order of the priesthood but had a few friends in the Salesian order. He spoke at length of himself, as if he was the one who had a story to tell. They ate together and had a glass of wine. He told Jonas that today was his day off and he had no specific duties regarding the parish, but a man of God was always on call. Jonas felt that the moment had come for him to drop his guard. He told his entire story to Father Henry according to his own interpretation. He could not tell for how long he spoke. He told about his shallow childhood and quitting school and selling drugs on the street corner where he eventually met the old man, who took him to a place called Pampuyo, where he learned and saw a great deal in a time incomparable to that of the passing of time on this Earth.

When Jonas finished his story it was pitch dark in the little house that the priest had behind the church. The priest stood up and turned on the light.

- Your story is very strange but not unique. I've heard of such places from different special people. They all had a similar experience as yours, but rare were those who gave that place the same name as you did. In my humble opinion we all have the capacity to visit such a place, but sometimes God himself sends you there. It is a rare privilege. Don't pass judgment on anyone who does not believe you. The Almighty decided on you for reasons that I will not question, and you should feel blessed about your experience over there if you want to call it that.

I can understand why you sense that there is more than you already knew. But one thing is certain; you know what your mission ought to be. However, we live in our world, with its laws and prerequisites. In order for you to pursue your calling, I will have to have you accepted in a seminary, where you will have to complete your academic studies and go on with the studies of the Order and all that follows. Tomorrow I will take you to them. I think it will be my part in the long road which lies in front of you. You are welcome to spend the night here. Tomorrow after the morning mass I will take you to Father Superior, along with my recommendations. And may God be with you.

And the priest kept his promise. The following day they departed for a long trip. After many hours they finally reached their destination.

THE LEARNING PROCESS

After following a long stone-paved road deep in the forest, they reached their final destination. The road ended on a vast domain that had on top of its gate the following words:

DUST TO DUST

A huge cross was placed above the words.

The domain was vast, with a three-story concrete building at its end. A few cottages were placed around the area. In the middle stood a big church with a cross on top of it. Not far away were what seemed a gymnasium and a stadium. Several students were either walking toward their classrooms or going about their duties. Others were farming a sizable piece of land and tending to herds of cows and goats. Some wore civilian clothes and others wore a gray robe. Somehow this place reminded him of a place he had been to not too long ago.

In the beginning Jonas kept mostly to himself, observing and being observed. The orientation office gave him a map of the site, his dormitory location, a rosary, a Bible, and a list of different things that he would need to collect at the mess. In reality it did not amount to much.

The seminarians were of different ages and races, he noticed. They carried on their faces a certain look of awareness that he liked. One of them walked toward him and wished him welcome. He said that his name was Tom, and he was assigned to make sure that Jonas knew about the place, the rules, his responsibilities, and his schedule according to the watch Tom handed him. He said that he should get acquainted with the map and the bells tones and numbers. Tom was about his age but appeared older for some reason.

Except for certain particularities, the place was like any ordinary big university, a place of learning. Jonas adapted himself quite rapidly to the system and was glad of the change of scenery too. He found solace in prayers and reassurance among the others. As the days went by, Jonas felt more reassured about his calling. His teachers were quite pleased with his wits and his thirst for learning.

Jonas spent four and a half years there. In retrospect he could not tell how fast time went by. The only certain thing was that he became a man of the cloth, about to become a full-fledged priest. Certain teachers left their imprints on him. There was one in particular, who taught theology and philosophy. His approach was somewhat original. Jonas tried to project his teaching by keeping the following in his mind. He said, reading the Old Testament is like watching a big motion picture about God, who used extravagance to make his people understand how powerful He is. He purposely put fear in their souls, and His wrath was unsurpassable. You could not hide from Him; He is the eye who sees everything. From Adam to Mosses, He made men learn the hard way. His exception was David and Salomon. His grandiosity could be matched by the shortness of the Chosen People. Miracles were the source of big motion pictures equal to the portrayals of Cecil B. DeMille.

Many who read the Old Testament saw a "bad-ass" God. His powers were exemplified through earth, wind, and fire. Nobody could question His dominion. Your only escape was in having unquestionable faith in Him. David and Salomon showed that there was a fatherly side of Him. His people could only bow to His principles. Then came Jesus, His Son. His entire precepts were based on freedom to choose and to love one another. He instilled in us what we can call *libre arbiter* (freedom of choice): the capacity of any human being to make the distinction between Good and Bad. He freed our minds to seek him and have faith freely. He showed us from rich to poor that everything was within our heart for learning and teaching while loving everything that represented an emanation of His Beloved Father.

The Bible in its entirety ought to be read historically, spiritually, and mystically. Jesus, with all his power, chose to live like the poorest of humans and at the end made the ultimate sacrifice by dying on the cross, begging forgiveness for the many things that we have yet to understand. He was tempted by the devil and once got very angry. Of all this, what is the big question regarding our own existence and our right to choose? Jonas thought, *If I were the one to write the Holy Book I would spend a great deal of time writing about Judas and the price of his loyalty. I would examine his inner self so deeply that one would say that I based all I understand about faith on loyalty rather than love. I would also make a drastic comparison to the state of our church nowadays. The teaching of Jesus Christ was so incomplete that he left to his disciples and a few of us to continue his work of love throughout the centuries until we meet with Him again.*

Jonas always carried with him the wisdom of his teacher. It helped him a great deal in his own journey.

THE VATICAN

At the end of his studies there, a few months later his class was ordained. Six of them received orders to pursue special studies in Rome. Father Superior told Jonas and the others that the Vatican had decided to enroll them in this special program. Like the others, his most valued possessions were the wooden cross and the rosary he received.

In spite of his modest upbringing in the streets, Jonas had led a sheltered life, and he had only a vague idea of the rest of the world. The trip to Rome was not pleasant. He was not very comfortable in planes. And it was a long trip. The Vatican was a big, luxurious place that did not fit with his learning. The opulence of Saint Peter did not, in his mind, reflect his vows of poverty and simplicity. His first few days were solely dedicated to touring the place and appreciating its grandiosity. They were housed and fed well and were at the disposal of their many guides. Jonas noticed many groups of priests going from one point to another, walking quickly and obviously very comfortable in their surroundings. They spent ten days like any other tourists. In his free time Jonas read again about Nero and his immediate predecessors and successors. He understood the historic use of Christianity for the greater good of Rome, and he saw how self-promotion could play a specific role in the growth of the Church. He remembered that one of his teachers had quoted, "Even God needs bells." To Jonas, the Vatican did not represent the words of wisdom and simplicity of Jesus Christ. Rather, it represented the need man had to display power and wealth.

Fortunately nothing he saw affected his faith; nothing he saw affected his inner soul either. On the contrary, he thought that through prayers understanding always came, and everything had its purpose on this Earth. If the Vatican were a simple shepherd's hut with a cross at its entrance, how many followers would Christianity, as a whole, have? Jonas did not relate his touring of the Vatican to anyone. What he knew he truly believed in and what he decided to accomplish were in the hands of God.

At the end of what he called a tourist vacation, they took the group to an isolated place, probably unknown to many, even though it was still part of the domain. They gave each of them a book of prayers and a rosary and told them classes were about to start.

THE POWER OF EVIL

That morning they all met with Cardinal Antonelli, who was accompanied by two bishops. Jonas later learned that one of them was responsible for the diocese where he would be sent. He was a frail man with piercing eyes. He asked all the classmates to take off their shoes and socks. One by one, he personally washed their feet. He began by saying, "You all have been selected to come here because the Holiness has decided to add several other courses to your curriculum. Our mission is difficult, but our faith is our helm. Yours will be even harder. You will be spending time taking child psychology courses and learning investigation tactics. As you are well aware, the Devil tries his best to corrupt as many souls he can. Lately our Church has been the subject of many criticisms that affect the true mission we have dedicated ourselves to on this Earth. Although you are all priests and belong to different congregations, the group you are about to form will have only one mission: fight the Devil. We are men, and we have our faults, but we took the vow to repress those imperfection in order to guide the less fortunate to the right path of God with the help of His son Jesus Christ.

"You are aware that many of us have been accused of being pedophiles and other abominations related to that type of ungodly behavior. Unfortunately, this is only the tip of the iceberg. Many other plagues, including drug trafficking, are infiltrating our churches in many parts of this world. You are about to submit yourselves to a grueling two-year training. The purpose of this will be to go back to your respective congregations and alone be the eye that sees everything. You will have an investigator as your personal contact, and you will never divulge your true identity to anyone. It is about time that we start cleaning up as many unwanted situations that we may encounter within our own house. I have to let you know that the Church has lost many priests, who were lured by temptations and other ungodly matters. My sons! The Devil has always been powerful, but no matter what, we must have the last word. It is our most sacred mission. May God be with you all!"

They understood clearly that on occasion they might serve as the extended arm of a police department. Probably a protocol was long before established between the two entities. Things were taken care of with caution and professionalism to reduce the number of scandals that might have happened if they were not meticulous.

Jonas spent hours relating to the training that they received. One thing was certain—each of them developed a second sense that told them that in certain situations prayers were not the only thing needed to get to the bottom of a problem.

There are defining moments in anyone's life. Jonas felt that he was about to enter one of these moments. And evil would not prevail.

DOING THE RIGHT THING

Jonas was assigned as the prefect of discipline of Saint Peter of Compassion, a fairly large parochial school for boys not far from where he grew up, though far enough away not to have been exposed to the activities of the inner city. In a way he could say that he was almost in charted territory. The school was within the diocese of the archbishop but was under his direct scrutiny as far as its curriculum was concerned. They had rules to follow, in accordance with both the precepts of the Church and the department of education. The teachers were all Salesian priests. The first item of order was to meet the entire faculty and staff. They were all ages, a few quite old. At twenty-six years old, Jonas looked as he always had, except that his face had matured and he now had more piercing eyes. As in other places, a few people looked at him with skepticism and others with disdain, as if he did not have the looks for the job.

It was not a coincidence that the prefect of discipline was a young man, since the job was very demanding. Jonas had over him a priest who everybody called Father Superior. They met on a regular basis, but nothing out of the ordinary ever came of their collaboration. Aside from keeping discipline per se, he was also obliged to oversee the curriculum of the school with his staff and get to know the file of every single student. They came from different backgrounds but were affluent. His office was a glass birdcage overlooking the entire playground. The priests' dormitory was in another part of the campus, not far from their small church. They all had individual cells, but Jonas had a set of keys for the entire facility.

Since Jonas's return from the Vatican, he'd been experiencing remorse. His soul was not at peace for many reasons. One was that he was not praying the way he used to, and the other reason had to do with the spy mission. There was a constant battle within his soul regarding mankind and the miseries people brought upon themselves. He believed in the love that could alter so many things. However, the scientific part of his mind undoubtedly knew that anywhere there was a positive was also a negative. That explained why in a way he loved math and physics so much. Mathematics was the universal language; Jonas could find no way any person could call him an atheist. The entire universe was filled with the hand of almighty God. Jonas found believing in Him was the easiest thing anyone could have asked of him. Dealing with human beings was a totally different case. He sought strength in prayers and contemplation. And now he had accepted a task that he did not know if he would have the guts to face and report on without the shadow of a doubt. It was so easy to point a finger at someone and irreparably affect the course of a life. They had been so quick to condemn Jesus Christ out of political fear and misreading his parables; they were so quick to praise Rome instead. In the name of the sword and power, so many miseries were provoked, and he knew all too well that words spoken without thought could be damaging. He prayed all the time. It became second nature for him because he always held in his mind how much we do not know about God.

All of the students were boarders. Their parents were diplomats, busy rich people, or famous actors. Jonas reflected on the fact that those people took the time to have these children but left most of their upbringings to others. Jonas knew all too well what it was to grow up without a parental presence and the warmth of a teasing father or a caring and loving mother. His heart and prayers went to these youngsters. He hoped to contribute, to the best of his abilities, to make this stage of their lives a positive and memorable one. Jonas already knew that the task awaiting him would never be easy. They would learn, grow up, and attend the best colleges and universities available. But the question always lingered somewhere along the way: would there be love? How would he define the haves and have-nots?

He was impressed by the lines of limousines dropping off these fragile creatures with only a peck on the cheek and a "see you on your next vacation." And then they were greeted by a bunch of man in dark robes who would become for many years to come their safety nets against the many challenges that were awaiting them. At least they were comfortable and well treated. All the classrooms were spacious and well lighted. The reputation of St. Peter went way back, and the screening to get into the school was incomparable. All the parents said that they were devout Catholics. Jonas made himself a note to recheck what *devout* really meant.

Jonas spent time reviewing each and every file of the schoolboys and sorted them according to their general psychological profiles. What the faculty members did not know was that he had also a file on every one of them and their human preferences, although they were supposed to have none. He had several meetings with the priest-teachers, and he truly listened more than he spoke, trying to assess every one of them. Their mannerisms and body language were more important to him than the words coming out of their mouths. His street background, never forgotten, helped him a great deal. He sensed that a few of them were not quite comfortable with him, and they referred a great deal to Father Superior, as if to remind him what his place was within their community. If there was one strength Jonas had, it was that he understood quickly what people around him were trying to convey. This was part of his survival process that brought him to where he was now. In light of all the unspoken messages, he just smiled and prayed. He found revival in his cell at night and in the prayers that became like a constant conversation with God. As the years passed him by, there were many things that he wished he could change, but he learned how to keep his mouth shut and accept the power of praying. He knew that moments that would test him were approaching very fast; he just sensed it.

Every morning they went to mass before regular school hours. This was the only time that the children were left alone, without the presence of a priest in their dormitory, though they had an in-house nanny who served as a mother figure within the community. What they did not know was every single one of them were nuns.

His everyday duties started routinely. The little incidents registered were no cause to be alarmed in any case. Jonas was getting used to the children and vice-versa. Keeping up discipline did not mean that he had to carry a big stick and make them afraid of him; this was not a prison for dangerous criminals but a privileged school. Although uncomfortable with it, his main task in the school never left his mind, but he prayed every day that he would never have to face such a degrading situation.

Life has a way of taking you by surprise in the least expected of ways. One day a brawl happened in one of the classrooms, and one of the students broke his companion's arm. Sometimes these growing males had to let some steam off, but since in that particular case there was an injury, the school asked the parents to present themselves as part of the disciplinary process and to avoid any liability against the institution. In a way it was routine. Jonas, along with the teacher in charge when the incident happened, received the parents, who were quite annoyed that they had to leave whatever they were doing to hear about a brawl that involved their children. Everything went according to the school rules, but during the conversation one of the parents was practically staring at Jonas. He did not recognize the man, but something told Jonas that they had met before. When the meeting was over they all left, but the man in question gave him an inquisitive look. Two days later Jonas received a formal written invitation to the bishop's office at an exact time. When he was invited to the bishop's office, the same man was already inside. Jonas automatically sensed that something important was about to unfold. The bishop, with an annoyed expression on his face, came right to the point.

- Mr. Davenport is quite disappointed with us because of your presence in his son's school.
- How so, Your Excellency?
- Mr. Davenport claims that he knows you from way back, and your place should not be in our school. I told Mr. Davenport that we have your entire file, but he insisted on having this meeting because of your past reputation.
- Where did we know each other, Mr. Davenport?
- Don't you remember me?
- I dare say no, but I'm sure that you are going to refresh my memory. I am all ears.
- When I was young I did some foolish things, like I told our bishop, and I used to buy drugs from you.
- The Church, as his Excellency told you, has my entire file, including information about the time I spent doing some foolish things myself, like selling drugs in a street corner.

- Nonetheless, I feel very uncomfortable seeing you in such a distinguished school, to which I am a major donor.
- Mr. Davenport, at the risk of displeasing you, I was sent to this school. I will go where the Church sees fit to send me.
- Do you mean by that you are a changed man?
- Probably, just like I hope to God that you no longer indulge in your past unfortunate habits.
- I am a changed man.
- I could not say the same for me except every moment of my life I pray to God for forgiveness and guidance, hoping that my prayers have reached our Savior. Do you pray, Mr. Davenport?
- Yes, every day.
- I encourage you to continue, because that's what saved me from many things. I also encourage you to carefully read about Saint Paul, who unfortunately did not have the privilege to meet with Christ in person. I'm certain that your son is in good hands— probably less than if he were with his parents, but we do our best to give all of our children the best we can offer. I am certain that His Excellency preceded my words, and all with the help of our God.
- You are very eloquent.
- Only my heart and my soul can express my gratitude for having gotten where I am now. Your presence here with us is a message that I still have much to do.

Whatever Davenport wanted to accomplish did not generate the fuel he needed to burn the hated feeling of his past misgivings toward Jonas. There would not be any inquiry. The bishop excused Jonas, and he left as he came, in all simplicity. Jonas was not made of ice, and the reminder of his past brought some disturbing memories, like the wasted life of his mother and the hypocrisy that he had to confront all too many times.

Jonas had his own way to pray when he was alone. He sensed that he could openly talk to God, and somehow he always knew that he was listening. Davenport did not face him, but he faced God's work through a simple man like him, a man who used to say that he was a nobody. Looking at his own life so far made him reflect seriously on death. Somewhere along the way he died to be born again; no matter how one looks at death, it is a transitory process that takes you to a higher level. *Dust to dust* concerned only the vehicle called the body. Lately people had been talking of the end of times and the catastrophes that would come along. Based on archeological discoveries, they even set an exact time for that occurrence. By doing so they dismissed the universal design of our almighty God. Look what happened to him with Davenport. It was a good thing. It reminded him that in spite of the dynamic of going forward, no one should ever dismiss his or her past. On the contrary, the past can only make you better if you are willing to make the proper corrections. A man with no history is a man with no identity.

Saint Peter of Compassion was a very good school for the elite. Jonas knew that the Salesians had other schools throughout the world that were more focused on educating poor children, and he hoped that someday they would promote him to one of them. Every day he made sure to accomplish his duties with all the precautions his position demanded. Each day he selected a group of children to focus closer attention on, especially in the courtyard when they were on their break. They were so full of life, so eager to look older and manlier. Of course there were the usual bullies and their continuous victims, but nothing out of the ordinary happened most of the time. They were just children growing up to become the responsible adults that society was expecting. However, one day Jonas's attention went to a boy who was spending too much time by himself, aloof and sad. Apparently something was bothering him, and Jonas wanted to know what it was, since none of the other children seemed to pay attention to him either. As if it were nothing, Jonas approached the kid slowly and sat by his side and said hello. At first the child looked uncomfortable, but once he realized that Father Jonas was not about to disturb him, he relaxed a bit. Jonas then asked him his name and walked away.

Each student attending St. Peter had a psychological evaluation in his file. They were done properly by an independent psychologist who specialized in adolescents. A few files regarding some bullying incidents caught his attention. They were mostly children who were bipolar or had some psychological disorder, but among them a very few presented no particularities to trigger such a violent attitude. This was Stanley Avwens's profile. That particular evaluation revealed that Stanley was as normal as any kid could be, except that he was more developed than average for his age. No particulars really stood out in his examination, except that he enjoyed writing as a hobby and football as a sport. His grades were more than satisfactory, and he came from a family of four. His father was a banker, his mother a chemist, and an older sister was in college—very normal, except that they were very rich. Stanley's file was not part of the pile of special students Jonas deemed it important to keep an eye on. Surely some of those students came from homes where the parents were strange enough, in spite of appearances and wealth, to have a negative influence on their children, but Stanley was not part of that group. Nonetheless Jonas sensed that he had to keep an eye on Stanley.

DOING THE WRONG THING

Jonas kept on watching Stanley while doing his rounds of the playground, the courtyard, and at times the classrooms. It was not unusual, due to his position, to roam any place he saw fit just to see how the kids were doing. He happened to see Stanley speaking to one of his teachers when he should have been on recess. When Jonas saw them in the hallway outside of the classroom all alone, the priest talking to Stanley looked rather disturbed. Jonas walked by as if it were nothing at all. The Church for too long had been trying to handle certain matters in a conciliatory way, hiding many embarrassing situations from the parents and the public as a whole. This was one of the reasons that for decades many scandals put the Church in a very undesired position that cost it distrust, money, and shame. Children are like small shrubs, and education and guidance are the supports that would allow most of them to grow straight, into normally developed adults. Like water is to the correct blossoming process of many natural beings, faith and prayer are the same to the spirit and the soul. Rare are those, Jonas thought, who have the opportunity to find God in their twenties nowadays and embrace that as the true blessing it was. A crooked small seed would probably not make it to a mature plant from which Nature can find the nourishment that would enable it recycle itself again and again. All educators have the solemn responsibility to facilitate good growth; a spoiled seed is the crack in the system that the Devil looks for in order to infiltrate his venom. Jonas thought that might fit into what he was so afraid could be happening to this young adolescent… He hoped that he was wrong about any premonitions he might have had because of his stay at the Vatican and the many things he read. He also wished that nothing of that sort would happen under his tenure in the institution. Whatever his thoughts may have been, his observations on Stanley indicated that he had to ask the kid in a gentle manner what exactly was wrong with him. Jonas decided that his first line of questions would have to center on him not playing with his friends. Gradually from there he would have to make the boy comfortable enough so he would open up to him about what exactly was disturbing him. Jonas concluded that this would be the best approach.

The congregation had its regular chaplain, but from time to time during the morning mass one of them might be chosen to do the sermon of the day. The topic Jonas picked was who they were as priests within the Church and as educators within the school. He spoke at length on guidance and protection. In a way, he meant to express a warning against any ill-guided authority an adult, whoever he may be, might have on youngster. From the looks he saw from the attendees, he believed that he touched a very delicate nerve, and truly he did not care one bit. He would not hinder any truth from coming out into the open under his watch. If there was a guilty one among them, he had better know that he had been warned. There were no words to say how fed up he was with all the hidden secrets in the Catholic Church. He knew that he could not change the world in order to make it a better place to live in prayers and glorying in God sincerely and openly, but that would not stop him, because for sure there were more good apples than bad ones.

Stanley remained his concern, and Jonas was determined to get to the bottom of his behavior. As the days went by, he sensed that he was gaining a certain trust from the child. One day, instead of talking to him openly, Jonas asked him to come by his office because he had something to ask of him. From his office, anyone could see the open grounds, so there was no place to hide. When Stanley came, Jonas put on his most amicable face and got right to the point.

- Stanley, I'm glad to see you. I meant to talk to you. Whatever we say here will have no effect on you or your attendance at the school.
- What do you want to say, Father?
- Lately I've been watching you, and apparently you've changed quite a bit. You should know that one of my main duties is to protect you—do you know that?
- Yes, Father Jonas.

- I cannot offer you confession, but I have to ask, Stanley—in your heart do you feel you have sinned?
- I guess so.
- Alone or with someone here?
- With someone here.
- Can you tell me who?
- I'm afraid, because he told me it was a secret between him and me.
- Stanley, no secret can be a sin.
- I did something with Father Claude.

What the child did not know was that everything he was saying was being recorded, which was why Jonas could not take his confession. What Stanley told him was sickening. Stanley had been molested and abused by Father Claude. All the details were on that recording. Now Jonas had another big problem—how to go about this. The first thing he had to do was to inform his superiors—not Father Superior at the school but Cardinal Antonelli and his staff. They were the ones to instruct him what to do. The only thing he could do while awaiting their instructions was to have Stanley avoid any personal or hidden contact with Father Claude. He told Stanley what to do not to attract any attention regarding the man, and he reassured him that he was not the one at fault. They prayed together, and Stanley left his office.

Any animal has a natural instinct that tells it that something is wrong or that it is in danger. The night after his meeting with Stanley, Jonas saw Father Claude speaking to a few other priests. As soon he walked by, they all shut their mouths. This raised an even darker thought in Jonas's mind, which was whether Stanley's misfortune was common among certain priests within the community. Jonas could not ascertain a correct link between God's precepts and the realities of events he'd encountered almost his entire life. The Devil had found refuge and strength in the Church, a place that many would call His sanctuary. There was no way he could reconcile what had happened to that poor kid and the repercussions the foul act could have on his adult life. Claude could not have been praying with the same openness that Jonas tried for.

Everything that man touches has a flaw, an imperfection, granted, but by no means does all he touches make the thing improper or unacceptable. Man has his flaws, but he also conveys greatness and good deeds. When they took their oath, it was a serious matter in the face of God, in spite of all the material attractions. Jonas was sad but not confused.

He'd sent his report through the proper Vatican channels, so he was not worried over any indiscretions. He was not surprised when they came and took Father Claude away to an unknown location without contacting him. The only thing that Jonas knew was that Stanley looked better. So far, he could not say that there had been any repercussions.

One night he was leaving the chapel to go to the priests' dormitory when he was cornered by four men, who gave him a beating he was not ready to forget. He got the message and remembered the beating that drug dealer gave him when he told him about his future intentions. That this happened to him now on very different grounds only showed him that men needed to do a great deal of searching in order to accustom themselves to the real precepts of Jesus. The following day he went to the doctor and found out that he had two broken ribs. He sent another report to the cardinal and requested a transfer to a less sophisticated place where he would be more at ease doing what he'd originally entered the priesthood for. He received a very long letter from the cardinal; at the end he promised Jonas that he would get his wish.

But before he left, several priests were either transferred or plain disappeared, just like that. Jonas realized that wherever they'd taken Father Claude, not only was he singing like a peacock about his misbehavior but also the Church was not about to get into the ugly mess that had smeared its reputation the last few years. He only hoped that whatever they did, they sought God's guidance and forgiveness. In reference to the beating he received, Jonas tried to find a common denominator between the gangs he used to cross paths with and this group of so called holy men. He realized that man in general is a social animal, with a definite awareness of their territory. Do not cross them unless you are willing to pay the consequences. Everything was created in a violent way, and for one to be and stay wise, a pacifist must transcend the basic elements of his making. This was the path that he chose, and he well knew that it wouldn't be easy. Even Jesus once let his anger gets the best of him at the temple, when he was chasing after those who tried to make this sanctuary a marketplace. He must always make sure that he would not defect from his calling, no matter what he would have to endure. He should never knowingly do the wrong thing.

THIS IS MY BLOOD, THIS IS MY BODY

Without a shadow of a doubt, Jonas knew that his companions in Christ saw his bruised face and his limping walk, but no one bothered to ask him what happened to him. He felt a surge of anger spread all over his being; he prayed relentlessly to overcome this somber conclusion. Yes, he prayed, mainly for those who'd caused him harm and discomfort.

Easter was approaching, and they were all in prayer mode. Jonas was among the saints of the Church if one would limit his appreciation by the expression of their faces. Their demeanor was for Jonas an acknowledgement of his role regarding the last events that systematically their well-oiled community of "holy" men.

Another aspect of Stanley's misfortune was that the kid apparently so far had never said one thing to his parents. He'd kept all the unfortunate experiences to himself. Jonas wondered what could be going through his mind. If one were to read about anyone's faith during this Easter season, many questions would be raised. Jonas knew through his readings that in the Qur'ân they considered Jesus only as a great prophet and do not allow the symbolism of the Holy Trinity. For that faith, Islam meant the conscious and peaceful obedience and submission to the will of the only God, Allah. Furthermore, it was said that Jesus did leave his own scriptures and they were lost. The basis of the Catholic Church is better based on Paul's legacy.

Knowledge is a good thing to have when you are able to accept your own path according to your free will before an established faith. Jonas accepted becoming a priest freely; he was not raised as a Christian or anything else, nor had he been exposed to any type of influence that could be connected to his final choice before he met that old man. Even then, the old man had never told him what he should do with his life. But when anyone freely accepted a path and misused it to bring harm and corruption to fragile minds, damaging the core of the expected growth of those youngsters. That was a crime. The mind needs to wonder and search freely, with guidance; suggestion is not an imposition, and opinions are not orders. Jonas had the privilege to come freely to God in spite of an unpromising upbringing. However, misrepresenting the responsibilities and moral duties bestowed upon a priest was for Jonas, and hopefully for many others, something demeaning and reprehensible. Children should be a crystal receptacle in which adults pour only what is best for them, in light of the challenges that are awaiting them. Jonas considered himself very lucky that he felt so comfortable with the path that he chose for his life. That was one of the reasons that, in addition to praying for Stanley, he also prayed for Father Claude. Of the two, he was the one needing more forgiveness for the harm that he had caused. Jonas did not once believe that he made the wrong choice of joining the Catholic Church. It just happened that recently it had been plagued with so many misplaced behaviors that came out of the open all at once. And they had to pay for all these lawsuits.

Jonas's head was full of unanswered questions, in spite of his years of study. He was ready to tackle whatever was awaiting him. His choice was made totally by himself in order to serve and rescue as many souls as God would allow him to, his own included.

Predicting what his future would hold was no concern of his. He had to take things one step at a time. In his mind, he felt like crossing a desert, ignoring the extremity. Something was lacking, and he could not put his finger on what it was. The only thing he was certain of was that he wanted no part of this school full of deserted rich children, but he also knew that his mission was to obey the Church and whatever decision that they made on his behalf. Jonas never wanted to be a priest who just went through the routine of using established prayers. Deep in his soul he always preferred to have a conversation with God. He found more peace when praying that way, without dismissing the community's prayers and the Gregorian incantations. There was something very uplifting when all the priests were singing, accompanied by a good organ player. Those things were food for the soul, and you did not necessarily have to be a priest to appreciate the impact. Unfortunately, coming back to the reality of his everyday routines were sometimes more difficult than other times. The path to faith is truly a challenging experience. So he waited, while giving his communion with God its utmost meaning.

THE DETOUR

No man can claim that his life never had any challenging moments. It would not be in the nature of one's passage on this Earth. Even when you have a clear choice that you made willingly, the negativity of certain realities tries to find a way to infiltrate your mind and taunt you.

In general, a priest does not live in a vacuum or in a place where his surroundings cannot affect his way of thinking. This is even more real when you serve a community of people with issues of their own, even though they are rich. One day, Jonas had to visit a public school to view a program they intended to establish to bring kids from all walks of life together so they could better understand that the world is not limited to their immediate acquaintances. In a meeting with a bunch of kids, the question of trust arose. Since Jonas was not the guest speaker, he had sufficient time to listen and watch body languages. He was so engulfed in his observations that he did not notice one of the children raise his hand and aim a question right at him. It took him a few seconds to realize that the child was directly talking to him.

- You are a priest, aren't you?
- Yes, I am a priest.
- Do you hurt children, or do you do funny stuff with them?
- I never did and never will. I am here to offer you my guidance and my prayers.
- I don't trust priests.

The other speakers went on to other matters, such as organizing a cookout by the lake, but Jonas never said one word after that brief exchange. That did not mean that he did not understand the source of the comment. Headlines like, SUSPENDED ROMAN CATHOLIC PRIEST PLEADS NOT GUILTY IN ALLEGED NATIONWIDE METH RING or BISHOP APOLOGIZES FOR ROLE IN HIDING PRIEST ABUSE were too common.

Jonas was quite aware of how many misdeeds went unnoticed in this world, but when it came to people holding public responsibilities, such things become just horrific. Until now, throughout his priesthood Jonas tried to never have bouts of anger because he knew all too well how anger could interfere with his true calling. However, lately he'd started to have serious thoughts about the Church. After so many centuries and years of meddling in matters that had nothing to do with the faith, the Church needed a complete overhaul, he realized. Jonas remembered all the commotion made about Too Big to Fail in the business world. The world of faith had a totally different dynamic and he knew that Rome was aware of it. They needed new blood, and nowadays young people shied away from anything and any principle that could interfere with a loose way to live. Something was missing. Could it be that the Church was being diverted from its true mission?

At a rather young age, Jonas had seen and learned a lot from coming from the gutter of existence. However, being part of a group of men and women who were supposed to devote their lives to helping others get closer to the true God left no place for so much corruption in his opinion. Rome truly had to reconsider its foundation and stop thinking that the Church was built from the ceiling to the floor. He would rather see the Church as a horizontal entity, with only minor vertical bumps to make the machine function properly. Like someone once said, it was easy to love but difficult to stay in love. Faith is like a well that never dries, he thought; the serious matter would always center on how long one's rope was, in order to draw nourishment for the soul.

Jonas continued his duties, giving the school the best of his capabilities as a man who'd seen so many things in such a short time. Certain questions continued to haunt his soul, and he found much solace in prayers.

Undoubtedly the Roman Catholic Church had gone through some difficult times lately, and the hard job of keeping the environment stable and free of any sinful, scandalous encounters was no easy task.

And to confuse matters even more, the pope declared that he was resigning from his holy office. His resignation rolled like a ball of thunder over the Church, considering how his predecessor endured all the physical hardships that were bestowed upon his body and certainly his soul. The question would always remain why, no matter what he said. Even the question of the vow of celibacy was again raised. Obviously, many questions were looming, putting the Church in a difficult spot. Nothing was lost in the translation of the pope's speech. It was very clear, without any confusion. For the billions of followers, including Jonas, this news came like a nuclear explosion.

Jonas felt that huge challenges were awaiting not only the pope's successor but the Church as a whole. Jonas blamed his vivid imagination, but shortly after this announcement an asteroid sped by the Earth's orbit, and a meteorite plunged down in Russia, causing a thousand injuries when it fell through a frozen lake. In the year 1413, the transubstantiation of the bread and wine into the Body and Blood of Christ came about. Under the consecrated bread and wine, Christ himself, living and glorious, became present in a true, real, and substantial manner: his Body and his Blood, his soul and his divinity (cf. Council of Trent).

At the present time there were 125 cardinals: sixty-seven Europeans, twenty-two from South America, fifteen from the United States, eleven from Africa, nine from Asia, and one from Oceania. This represented the powerhouse from which the next pope would emerge. However, one from Scotland had to present his resignation due to alleged sexual misconducts with several priests—students from some thirty years ago. Rumors were that the pope was retiring, more overwhelmed by disgust than physical fatigue. Deep in his soul-searching, Jonas came to terms with the idea that in this type of situation the messenger was as valuable as the message. Many people thought that the Church was not far from complete obliteration. However, his deepest thoughts indicated that big changes were about to come within the Church, and not necessarily those expected. The signs were unequivocal.

In his personal revival, Jonas wondered why he had to choose the Catholic Church in seeking his spiritual rebirth. He could have chosen another path. Not believing in coincidences, he was certain that God did not make him make the choice lightly and that he would certainly find the reason out, probably with no personal effort.

Talk of openly gay marriage was on the lips of many who in Jonas's view did not quite understand the necessities of chastity and celibacy. For Jonas it was never a question of sacrifice but better yet a question of accommodation. When anyone was involved in a loving relationship, that person had to find the time to nourish such involvement. Those were commonly called obligations, and there was nothing wrong with that as long as you were available at all times, even when resting. People actually made a big thing out of nothing. It was not given to everybody to serve with joy at any moment and at any time. It was as simple as that.

More than ever, with all the news surrounding the Catholic Church, Jonas, the little drug pusher turned priest, found a calling to make thing better. In his small ways, he must reestablish the correct connection between the teaching of this holy man and the bunch of pageantry of all sorts that were driving away the simplicity and the purity of this *true teaching*. Bigger days were coming for the Catholic Church, he was certain of that. However, there would be no place for cowardliness, less hypocrisy. This was just a detour, just a distraction for the souls who thought they had reached a level of holiness and self-righteousness, as if those things were bestowed just because you were advancing in grades and ranks among the community of priests. Peter, the man who denied Christ twice, was the chosen one upon whom He decided to build His Church. The simplest prayer to God was when you opened your heart and spoke your mind without any hang-ups. Jonas believed that they had drastically affected the great awakening left by Jesus Christ, which was actually a philosophy based on simplicity, love, and understanding. In that early stage of his priesthood, Jonas feared that most Christians were confusing faith and religion.

Jonas continued his soul-searching while attending to his duties. What he feared the most was that all of the events and scandals would not affect the core of his own faith and the real mission of the men and women like him who decided this path to serve God. Through his readings and research, he knew that all creation has an element of violence; he would not have to go any further than the theory of the Big Bang. Jonas wanted to serve, and so he would, no matter what. He did not know what the future held for him, but so far his determination was not altered a bit by all those things. He thought that in itself was a good sign.

PEEPING TOM

Granted, Jonas never had any sexual encounters, but that did not mean that he was unaware of the things that can go on between two people, depending on their sexual preferences. The archdiocese hired two female teachers, which in a way was not unusual, but for some reason Jonas had certain apprehensions regarding this. Both women were young and beautiful. One was responsible for teaching etiquette and manners and the other speech and posture. Looking at the full curriculum of the school, there was no doubt that it was for the wealthy and no one else. The women's names were Eva and Patricia, and they seemed to enjoy the new assignment. However, Jonas had a funny feeling that they had just walked into a lion's den. Obviously they had specific schedules and at the end of the day went home to their respective private lives. However, their entrance into the close-knit teaching body of priests did provoke quite a stir. Jonas did not forget the biting attitude he had received from his colleagues and the beating he had received thereafter. He could even sense a few of them salivating over what they would do to these women. Jonas felt ashamed to have such negative thoughts, but he could not keep himself from having a premonition that their being here was another big mistake.

The women were assigned a room with its own toilet, completely isolated from the compound where the priests lived. That was a good thing, because in between classes they had a private place where they could rest or relieve themselves. Jonas was glad at least they were not in-house guests. Eva and Patricia, according to their files, were devoted Catholics and had previous experience with other schools like this one. They were very satisfied with their past experiences and so were their previous employers. In a word, they came highly recommended.

Months passed, and Eva and Patricia did not find it hard to blend within the small male community. They even cracked a few jokes from time to time with everybody except Jonas, but he was used to it. Because the guesthouse was not used very often, the women complained about some leaks within the place. As part of his duties Jonas was responsible for supervising the housekeeping and maintenance of the entire campus; it was part of his role in keeping discipline running smoothly. Jonas had an independent plumber come and take a look at the problem and took the occasion to personally supervise the repairs. He was familiar with the premises, which consisted of a full bedroom apartment with a small balcony—nothing fancy but comfortable enough. While Jonas was checking the plumber's work he noticed several glass circles, especially in the bathroom. When he got closer, he understood that someone had planted a few surveillance cameras in the apartment. The women were being spied on when they were using the facility. Jonas wondered why anyone would go that far in order to have a glimpse of a female counterpart unless he was basically a pervert.

The cameras were well hidden, and Jonas thought that the only reason he noticed them was because he was suspicious of everything ever since he'd worked in the streets, let alone because of the special training he had in the Vatican. Because he came and went routinely, he was certain that he did not draw anybody's attention. He finally discovered that the entire system was operated by remote control and was connected somewhere in one of his colleague's cells, if not several of them. To make matters worse, one day he found a picture of one of the women having a shower, and the picture did not leave anything to anyone's imagination about what she was actually doing while taking a shower. It was a vivid infringement on her privacy. Jonas was outraged, but he knew better than to pursue his investigation any further, not only for his own security but also out of disgust and procedures. Like Job, Jonas thought that God was focusing some nasty tricks on him in order to challenge his devotion to Him and the Church he freely chose to serve. He requested a meeting with the bishop, stating that he had some serious matters to discuss with him. His request was granted, and he went to see him.

The bishop was a very astute and careful administrator. He received Jonas in his office, his assistant armed with a notebook and a pen. The three men sat down, and after they prayed together and, the bishop offered Jonas a cup of tea and sat down and listened to his report while the other priest was taking notes. He asked Jonas several questions regarding the day-to-day activities at the school after the situation with Stanley. Jonas answered truthfully but was surprised when the bishop told him that he'd omitted telling him that he got bitten by a few of his comrades after the previous incident. Jonas just told him that he did not feel that the incident was that important, but he said that not all of his comrades were that bad or perverted. Jonas also took the opportunity to remind the bishop that several months ago he'd asked for a transfer and that he never received any answer. The bishop looked at him straight in the eyes and told him that his mission at the school was not yet over and that he should pray harder. Unequivocally and unmistakably, he was the joker in a game far beyond his understanding. The bishop did not offer any other form of encouragement. The man did not get where he was by pure accident. Jonas was above all part of the Church, which was enrobed in a hierarchy that encompassed all kinds of situations. When the bishop was seeing him out of his office, he told Jonas that he continued to count on his loyalty and his discretion.

Jonas spent the next few days reassessing the Church's code of ethics and all the scandals that were plaguing its holy mission. He thought of the old man and his strange trip to Pampuyo and felt privileged to have had that particular and peculiar experience. His mind was stuck on the meaning of freedom of choice and what prompted some men to choose the priesthood when there were so many ways to serve God. Like any other people, the priests also watched television in their free time, and very often they watched the news in particular, a way to stay connected with the world outside of their "bubble." The newscasters lately relentlessly had relayed some news about some priests involving their sexual orientations or deviations, certainly not leaving alone the civil rights of gays and lesbians. It became redundant and boring, but they were doing their job to report as much news that came across their desks. However, that did not mean that the media was on a witch hunt to hang the Catholic Church. Very rarely did they release news of an incident that was viciously overblown.

Jonas had a dilemma with his companions in Christ. When he was in his early teens he used to go with a couple of youngsters to watch pornographic movies, and they masturbated the living hell out of their privates. To think of it at that moment brought a smile to Jonas's face. But having adults going as far as to install spying apparatus so they can get some type of enjoyment out of it was no laughing matter. The ladies went on teaching their classes in the school, but the archdiocese decided to remove the ladies from the guesthouse and continue to ignore the surveillance equipment that was installed in it; they did this apparently on purpose. Whoever made that type of investment could continue watching the walls. Jonas again noticed a few dirty looks from some of the priests, but since he already knew that he was not "Miss Congeniality" among some of them, it really did not bother him a bit. Jonas knew that the bishop would get to the bottom of this indiscretion, and he would do so in the proper time. Jonas realized that administering to such a big body of people was not a simple matter, and the Catholic Church was very big and very sensible to manage. Just like the rest of the human world, they were not perfect, and there were a few bad apples who unfortunately always tried to have an entourage. Most of all, the Church was a social structure that at times suffered the attitudes of those who should not be in a position to be attracted by such degrading behaviors. Corruption can be a falsely attractive tool. The teaching of Christ showed the right path to God.

Jonas knew that he was not at the top of the mountain overlooking others' undoing. That only reinforced his commitment and will to pray even harder for himself, his companions, and the mission they all chose to accomplish. But like they say, all the above made Jonas have some personal thoughts regarding the Church he served to the best of his faith. He recalled his stay at the Vatican and the amount of wealth he saw there for the first time in his life. This memory still bothered him in relation to his own understanding and what he had been taught regarding the teaching of Christ, in all its simplicity. Having evolved, Jonas came to peace with all the elusive appearances. Although he used the term with a lot of apprehension, power had to be shown and felt. Keeping the reality just like the carpenter's son would not amount to all of this. Jonas was at peace with himself and did not feel any covetousness in the way he was accepting the Church. Those few perverts did not represent the real image of the Church with its 1.2 billion followers, with Africa offering many newcomers. Jonas was for obvious reasons concerned about the education they were imposing on these youngsters and hoped that they would keep their devious habits to themselves. It was unfortunate that because of them the Church had to spend millions and millions of dollars in order to prevail on those misdeeds. Jonas was at peace with himself so far, but he truly had some concerns. His thoughts went to a sermon given by the Reverend Leeroy Wilfred Kabs-Kanu, copastor of the covenant Child World Ministries, in which he stated:

> The most unhappy, grouchy, and temperamental person on this earth is the man or woman who is not self-content. On the flip side, the happiest person on this earth is the man or woman who is content with what he or she has. The Bible teaches authoritatively about this: let your conversation be without covetousness; and be content with such things as ye have: for He hath said, I would never leave thee, nor forsake thee.

One day the archdiocese sent workers to renovate the guest house. Jonas noticed a few men who did not look like maintenance workers. Without fuss, everything was removed and nothing was said. It was another lesson that

Jonas had learned. You can walk softly and accomplish the unexpected, knowing that the element of surprise would always be in your favor. However, Jonas was certain that as long as they didn't get rid of the perverts, they would find other means to make the Church look bad. So he braced for anything that he might stumble upon or find out by any unexpected means. God would always be with the just.

BE AWARE OF YOUR SINS

The life of any human being was never a simple walk in the park under a clear blue sky; that of a priest was even more complex, with an apparently boring routine. His life lays especially in its intellectual and mystical achievements and the need to serve. Knowingly that the Devil is always in the details, hiding in the bushes to better stalk his prey. Jonas was always on the lookout for him, he knew that the battle the Devil engaged in to gain human souls would never cease, regardless of many deceitful appearances.

It was a very clear day. The school was on recess and the students were all away somewhere in the world, likely with their parents. The vast facility was truly strange with them away on a short vacation, but everybody welcomed the rest. It was around noon when the police came asking to see Jonas. Automatically he knew that something was wrong, very wrong.

The investigator did not waste any time. He got right to the point after presenting his badge to Jonas.

- It's about Father Claude.
- What about him?
- A few days ago he was killed in the sacristy of his church.
- We did not know that. How very sad!
- He used to be here, right?
- Yes but he was transferred to another church.
- Do you know why?
- Have you talked to our bishop?
- Not really.
- You see, Inspector, I belong to an order, and anything I say or do has to have the seal of approval of my superiors. I hope you understand, especially in a case like this.
- I understand, and I will be back to question probably all of you.
- I look forward to see you again with the proper credentials.

The investigator left. Jonas felt sorry about the death of Father Claude, hoping that his violent death was not due to his downfall. Instinctively he prayed for his soul to the merciful and understanding God. His prayers for the deceased could not alter his fears that Stanley might have something to do with the priest's assassination.

Jonas knew that the investigator talked to other priests in the school, but strangely nobody mentioned anything to him. Jonas had never truly blended in with the group, and that had nothing to do with race or social origin. He believed there must be something about him that made the others feel uncomfortable with him. Having had a life in a difficult environment helped Jonas endure the challenges he faced in his vocation to serve. He knew that nobody was perfect. However, that did not mean that one should fly above the many temptations and problems that others were confronting. He made a note to himself to have a closer look again at Stanley's demeanor in order to detect anything that he might have missed. Jonas admittedly felt that he should not have any negative thoughts regarding that young man without having any information whatsoever about his involvement in what happened to that priest who had abused him.

Jonas waited but did not receive any call from the bishop informing him about what type of action to take when the investigator came back. One might think that nothing had happened; everybody went on doing whatever he was doing before that awful news. Even Stanley looked as natural as ever in his eyes, and he did not care to bring up any subject regarding this past experience, hoping that the youngster did not have anything to do with the murder. Finally he received a note from the bishop, telling him to fully collaborate with the investigation.

As predicted, a few days later the investigator came back to see Jonas. However, this time the mood of the conversation was more intense.

- How are you, Father?
- Well, by the grace of our Lord.

- The last time we met I neglected to tell you how Father Claude was killed. You did not ask.
- I believed that you would tell me when the moment was appropriate.
- Yes.
- So how was he killed?
- With a BB gun, three shots in the head. There were several knife wounds. The killer made sure that he was dead because he checked him out with his right shoe after he murdered him.
- How gruesome.
- We have certain indications that Father Claude was a child molester.
- Since I can freely talk to you, yes, he was.
- Do you know who exactly he molested while he was here?
- I know only of one case.
- Did you make a report regarding that case?
- Yes, and I sent it to my superiors.
- Rest assured, Father Jonas, that we will not use your report if it turns out to be irrelevant.
- I hope so.
- Do you believe that the child ever said anything to his parents?
- I believe that he did not.
- Can you give me a copy of the file?
- I was ordered to cooperate with you, but they did not tell me to give you any file. You will have to

contact my superiors, considering the delicacy of this case.

- I can understand that, but tell me, without compromising yourself, do you believe, based on your personal observations, that this student could do such a thing?

- Maybe. Maybe not, and that's an honest answer.

- Needless to say, the killer was pretty close in order to shoot the victim with such accuracy and knife him with such cruelty.

- Yes, I believe you are right.

- I hate this type of case for the simple reason that you have to do your job while understanding, as a parent, what might have been going through such a young person's mind. Nonetheless, the job has to be done, and the killer, whoever he may be, will have to face our judicial system. They are the ones who will decide what to do with him. All I can promise you is my absolute discretion.

- Thank you, Inspector. As you are well aware, our Church has been going through some difficult and embarrassing times lately. We do our best to cleanse ourselves from the evil deeds of a few bad apples. May God be with you. Do stay in touch.

- I will.

When the investigator left, Jonas felt an urge to pray for him. He probably was a parent too, a parent who entrusted part of his children's academic education to professionals he did not know much about. When they came home, the usual conversation would start with, "How was school today?" And he certainly hoped that everything went fine for them while the family routine went on. The youngsters at St. Peter were not as lucky. They belonged to an economic and social background that put them within the more fortunate, as if money and creature comforts could bring you everything. Their mission was also to instill in them the notion of God as part of their everyday lives, while encouraging them to do good deeds for the less fortunate. Finding priests with such a gratifying mission taking advantage of their situation to exploit sensitive souls was simply appalling and degrading. Jonas considered it to be a privilege to serve God on that level, and he still had difficulties acknowledging that these situations had been going on for as long as the Church was established. This was a question of human deviation when limited by some misinterpreted boundaries. Vice versus virtue: two poles of impossible correlation. All mankind had to live both between and with them.

This thing was not over yet. Jonas knew that the investigator was floating in a pond of delicate equilibrium between a murder and the Church's already tarnished reputation. Although he appeared to be having difficulties with this case, Jonas knew that the investigator was progressing slowly but surely. He also knew that he would have to see this investigator until the murder was solved and the suspect brought to trial.

Jonas never bothered to learn where exactly Claude was transferred to, but it must have been in a geographical zone under the diocese. During that time he cautiously tried to gain Stanley's trust, because no one told him that he was the prime suspect, let alone that he was among the suspects. However, just in case he would have to intervene, Jonas would rather that the youngster told him everything he knew instead of learning anything at first hand from the police. Jonas started by giving him small assignments regarding courtyard maintenance. This in itself was nothing new; from time to time one of the students was chosen for such duty in order to instill the sense of equality and respect toward the less fortunate.

Jonas was still searching for a way to interact with Stanley without making him feel that he was being taken out of his comfort zone. Eventually it came from him, not Jonas. The youngsters were allowed to have their own private time under light supervision. Many used that time to play, others to read, and the rest of them to interact on some type of social media. Who nowadays did not have a computer? Jonas's code name was just Jons, and he did not have that many followers, just a few with whom he kept regular chats on different subjects, mainly mathematics and physics. Jonas had kept the sciences as a hobby although he was so good at them in school. In school they had helped him a great deal to improve his general results to the utmost academic level.

One day he was on the Net when Stanley asked to be friends with him. From the profile he posted it was not hard for Stanley to recognize him. He purposely did not reveal his real identity or that he was the priest that he saw on a regular basis at his school. This omission was voluntary; you were not obligated to do so just because you wanted to belong to a specific group—that was one good thing about the social networks. They exchanged ideas and opinions on current events, but things really did not get too personal. However, from his questions Jonas could sense that Stanley liked to probe his partners, and he kept the same type of conversation with all who belong to his group. He did not request any privacy. Jonas noticed that the more they were interacting, the more he was beginning to see the real Stanley: a more sensitive person who was looking to define own personality in opposition to his famous parents, whom he barely saw. Stanley was the one who finally set the pace of the correspondence. Jonas did not want to make any mistake that could raise any suspicions.

One day after a long day supervising some midterm exams, he found this question on his chat:

- What do you think of people who abuse children?

After careful thought he engaged in the conversation.

- Do you mean reprimand or abuse? Because there is a difference.
- Yes! I mean abuse.
- Well, it is not right, because that kind of things can leave lasting consequences on the victim.
- I gather that you are older than me.
- Yes.

- Do you know that abuses most of the time are done by someone who is actually liked by the victim, and it takes a while for him to realize that this must not be part of a bonding experience?
- I was not aware of that.
- You see, once we like someone, in our minds he can do no wrong.
- It is part of trusting.
- Yes.
- Can you imagine the disappointment when he understands what has been going on?
- No.
- He feels that's his fault not his. The tendency is to forgive and forget, but once you get to that point it cannot leave your mind. It becomes a battle between what is acceptable and what is immoral.
- I believe that there are people who specialize in helping children and, for that matter, any young person in such a situation.
- It is not that easy to talk about such things.
- Did you speak to your parents?
- I did not tell you that I was the victim. As for my parents—well! Forget about them. I even wonder how and why they had me.
- Let's assume that you, in spite of everything, would have find a way to speak to them about such a delicate matter.
- They would think that I'm inventing things. I don't trust them because if they did love me as

their child, why would they put me away so I would
not be an inconvenience to their schedule and their
entertaining lives away from me?

- That's a harsh thing to say.
- Well! It's true.
- I believe I can help if you would let me.
- But you don't know me, Jons.
- I'm getting to, and my offer still stands and is
sincere.

The conversation stopped there, and Jonas concluded
that he just wanted to think about that. Jonas wondered
about what was going through his mind and how lonely he
must feel while dealing with this situation, which obviously
affected him to a point he felt compelled to talk to a stranger
about it. What a heavy burden for such a young mind!

Jonas went on with his daily duties with a sour taste in
his mouth. However, he knew for certain that the situation
just only begun. The only thing he could say for certain
was that Stanley's attitude had not changed in any way. Not
taking that for granted, he subtly continued his observations,
still hoping the boy had nothing to do with that gruesome
murder. By all appearances nothing had changed. As a
matter of fact, he noticed Stanley engaging more with his
fellow classmates.

The visit of the investigator changed Jonas's mood. For
apparent reasons, he was not too happy to see him again.
The man looked like a cartoon character trying to represent
the embodiment of the TV character Colombo. He was

like a weasel and never got to the point. In any case, he certainly was doing his job, not leaving any stone unturned. He greeted Jonas with a hypocritical smile that seemed to never leave his face. Again his visit was about Stanley. Now he wanted permission to meet with him and ask him a few questions. Jonas asked him why, and he answered unequivocally that he had reasons to believe that Father Claude had taken a particular liking to the boy. Jonas had no other choice than to summon the boy. He met them in an office where the investigator could question him to his satisfaction. He only hoped that would be the last time.

They spent quite a long time talking. Jonas was dying to know the tone and the evolution of this conversation. He personally did not like this investigator.

When he finally left, Jonas noticed that Stanley was flushed with anger and did not want to say anything about the conversation with the investigator. That night Jonas did not notice Stanley in the dining hall. His excuse was that he was indisposed and did not feel like eating his dinner. Jonas knew for sure that this had to do with his earlier encounter.

The following day Jonas did not see Stanley, and he did not answer to the usual attendance roll. Jonas contacted his floor surveyor and had his room opened. Stanley was gone, nowhere to be found. Worse, Jonas could not call his parents because they were on a documentary tour somewhere in Africa.

INNOCENT UNTIL PROVEN GUILTY

It was, to say the least, a very delicate situation. The first initiative Jonas took was to present the full situation as he saw it to the bishop, who in turn told him to contact the investigator, who was not supposed to talk directly to Stanley unless there were no alternatives, and even so, the bishop had to be notified. Obviously the bishop was not too happy about the unraveling of this so-called investigation. Jonas felt that he took the situation very hard, and he said to Jonas that he thought that this situation certainly would cost the Church one way or the other in the near future. Jonas could not have agreed more.

It was not a surprise to see the investigator again, and Jonas, quite disturbed, asked him what exactly he said to Stanley. He acknowledged that Stanley was not too talkative, and he sensed that Stanley thought that he was considering him as a suspect in the murder of Father Claude. And he did not make any bones about the fact that, yes, he suspected him, along with many other students, due to the gruesome manner in which he was killed. Apparently he'd received several knife wounds and had his testicles cut off.

The archdiocese instructions were short but specific: Jonas had full responsibility to cooperate with the authorities as long as the Church was kept at bay during this scandalous development. Even from a human point of view, let alone a Christian way, Jonas felt let down in this ordeal. Could it be that the hierarchy was already that scared, even though this wasn't the first scandal? Therefore, they should know better than he how to deal with such a situation. But above all, Jonas was a man of God with heavy responsibilities, given the fact that his immediate obligations were to young children. His own faith was telling him that he could not just let this remain solely with the proper legal authorities. He simply cared; his first, urgent priority was to find Stanley. However he felt obligated to personally get in touch with his parents. With the State Department's help, he finally got in touch with Stanley's parents, learning that only the mother was able to fly back to see if she could be of any assistance. Something seemed to have snapped in that kid's mind, and Jonas prayed to God that it did not cause too much damage.

Jonas had never prayed so much in front of his computer. He stayed online and waited for Stanley to at least start chatting. He was not a serious user of social networks, but he knew that most students were. So he started making himself more available on the Net, hoping that his efforts would not go unanswered. He even posted prayers under the pseudonym of Jons. God only knows how long he waited before the beep of an incoming message awakened him.

- Hello, Jons, hope you are well.
- I'm fine—how about yourself? Been missing you.
- I am away and hiding.
- Why?
- Some people think I killed somebody.
- Do they have any reason to think that?
- Yes, but they are wrong.
- So why are you hiding?
- Because I should have been the one to kill him.
- Who is *him*?
- Someone I knew, the one who molested me.
- I understand, but I disagree.
- I have a feeling that I know who you are, Jons.
- Would you trust me any less?
- No, Father Jonas.
- You are very smart.
- I believe so.
- What should you and I do about it?
- Very soon, if we continue chatting, they will trace me to you, and that would put you in a very difficult position.
- Your mother is coming.
- If you know how to talk to her, she will reveal where I am without her even noticing it. I need to talk to you, but you will have to find me before the police do. Good-bye.

- We have to talk.
- We will.

Stanley's mother arrived on a late flight. The following morning she was already at the school seated in front of Jonas's desk, as anxious as ever. She was a strikingly beautiful person, but she seemed detached and unreachable in spite of her presence in that office regarding her son's running away. Jonas did not have a lot of practice dealing with women, be it a prostitute like his mother or a high-class lady who certainly was disturbed about leaving a daily routine with her husband on that faraway continent. According to what he gathered from her, both her husband and she came from money and high-standard Catholic pedigree upbringings. They met at the university; they were both anthropologists with special background studies in African tribes and customs. This incident interrupted them from a documentary they were making for a nonprofit organization that wanted to learn about the source and development of the brutal African ritual of castration. Jonas thought how very funny that was, considering Father Claude had suffered, before or after his death, a similar fate.

Because of their busy schedules, Stanley spent most of his time with the same nanny who had taken care of his mother when she was a child; she had complete trust in her. Due to their upbringing they found it suitable to enroll Stanley in a school that responded to their expectations, but it seemed that they could have been mistaken. Jonas did not like her posture and the tone of her voice. She was condescending, to say the least, and left the impression that Stanley was more of an accident than a planned endeavor. She wore no wedding ring but wore plenty of jewelry to show her opulence. Jonas decided not to get into any details with the woman but told her that the police were conducting their investigation. Because of Father Claude's tenure at this school and his revealing past, they were compelled to get in touch with all parents whose child had had any type of involvement with the cleric.

Everything that she told Jonas was recorded. Jonas asked her if she would see any problem with him talking to Stanley's nanny. She was more than willing to call her and make an appointment for her to come and see Father Jonas. After that, she spoke a while of the time they used to spend with Stanley in her husband's great-uncle's farm and how tiring it was for her to go horseback riding on so many acres of land. Jonas gratefully thanked her for coming and noticed a slight hint of motherly concern when she asked him to protect and find their son before the police did.

Jonas felt that he'd failed Stanley, he should have moved faster. Maybe it would have prevented him from doing anything wrong or foolish. He prayed to God to keep the boy safe and sound, knowing that he must be feeling alone and unloved. Jonas became a priest because he'd had the calling, indescribable to any other human who had not lived through that experience. However, he felt a deep emptiness over not serving as he'd anticipated. He still believed that he should be the type of priest who had no home besides all the places he had to go spreading the good precepts of the Lord.

He wanted to save souls, saving his own in so doing. Maybe this was too presumptuous on his part. Maybe he was trying to dictate to the Lord the path upon which he should have already put him. Maybe he was not yet as humble as he thought. He prayed and fasted, looking forward to meeting with Stanley's nanny. He'd already braced himself against any unsatisfactory outcome.

The nanny was a middle-aged lady with mild manners and a soft voice. But beneath it was easy to notice a strong will and a determined opinion regarding the children who grew under her guidance. She had very strong view about Stanley and a low opinion regarding his parents. Jonas related his last conversation with the mother and the exchanges he'd had with the young man. He was not surprised when she told him that Stanley had wanted him to find him. He was on the right track.

Before leaving to look for him, Jonas spoke officially to the others. He knew that all of them were aware that another scandal, if not handled properly, was about to tarnish the Church. This time he found a very conciliatory audience. Jonas left in the early hours and, following the map, had no problem reaching the farm after a short drive. The place was fully staffed, with a relative serving as a supervisor. He told Jonas that he was a cousin and that Stanley's mother had called him to let him know of his forthcoming visit to the farm. Jonas concluded that she had known exactly where the boy was but for their own reasons did not get in touch with him. That made him wonder about certain families' structures and habits. To his mind, something was missing.

After identifying himself to the person in charge, Jonas was escorted to a barn, where he found Stanley on a stack of hay reading a book. When he saw Jonas, he stood up and greeted him cordially. He was obviously relieved that things had gone according to how he'd wanted. Without further ado, he started talking to Jonas about Father Claude's conduct toward him, without omitting any details. Jonas was certain that he did this on purpose. It was reassuring to see the young man in such good spirits, although he looked slightly thinner than the last time he'd seen him. Jonas listened to his confession, although he was not the one at fault, and then he started the conversation that had brought him all the way there to look for him.

- You know that the police are inquiring about the students who were under Father Claude while he was at the school, including you?
- I did not kill that man, but I'm glad that someone did. I came here to put my head together about why so many things have happened to me since I was born and why my parents had me, since I don't have any value for them. I'm just a mistake.
- No human being is a mistake, Stanley, no matter how complicated or difficult his life may be.
- Did you know that my parents are no longer together? Their last argument happened before my eyes, and it had to do with me. My father went through an elaborate speech about how their marriage was a

mistake, that when my mother became pregnant they had me because of their religious beliefs.

- They could not say all of these things in front of you.
- They did not know that I was by the stairs, listening to them arguing.
- That's unfortunate. Too many times people tend to say things that they don't mean out of anger.
- So tell me—how come they both have lovers while keeping this façade of a marriage?
- How do you know all this?
- Because my father's mistress is the maid, and my mother's lover is the chauffeur. We are so twisted that we look as if we came out of some cartoon for adults. And I'm right in the middle of that comic farce.
- What you are telling me is indeed very disturbing. I have to take your words as a solemn truth.
- You are beginning to understand why I am an inconvenience to them and why I intend to render them a good service.
- How?
- By killing myself.
- That would be a big mistake. It would say that you have no feelings for your parents in spite of their misbehaving. By the way, don't you know that you may have a big challenge to bring light and harmony to your family? God is in all of us, Stanley, but some people need help, and only He knows where this

help will come from. Do you know where your parents are?

- Somewhere in Africa.
- You just told me that they are not harmonious with each other.
- But I never told you that away from me they are able to work together, especially because they both enjoy it and make a lot of money from what they are doing.
- I gather that they are both anthropologists.
- Yes, but I believe in separate fields that can be related. I'm not too sure, but sometimes they are in different parts of the world at the same time. That makes me wonder when exactly they had time to have me, since it happens that one is at home and the other away.
- An odd couple, but it does not mean that they do not have feelings for each other.
- Maybe. They are both well published. Even the library at school has their writings. My mother uses her maiden name, so their marital status often goes unnoticed.
- Do you have a BB gun?
- No, but we have shotguns on the farm. I'm a good shooter, even better than my father.
- So you do spend time with him?
- Of course, but not like you would consider in a regular family.

- Don't you think that you are being too harsh on them? I met your mother the other day.
- How come?
- When I finally reached them to inform them you were missing, she left her work and flew all the way back to talk to any authority that needed her help to find you. That sure does not look like a person who does not give a damn about you. While she was with me your father called to find out any new developments.
- But she did not even bother to come to the farm!
- Maybe when you see her, you can ask her that question. I'm not here to judge your parents. I'm here to convince you to come back with me and face everything like a man instead of running away from reality, no matter how difficult it can be at times. By so doing, along with some deep soul-searching and my help, you probably will find out that you may have misjudged your parents, in spite of their imperfections or sins.
- You are very convincing, but there are certain things that you don't know regarding my parents, and in any case that is not the purpose here.
- You are right. Let me take you back to the school.

Stanley gave him a long look in which Jonas could detect a great deal of sorrow and confusion in that young mind. However, he also sensed relief in this look, as if to say, someone does care about me.

Stanley walked with him back to the house and picked up the clothes that he had taken with him. He told Jonas that he was ready. The ride back was very quiet. Stanley was listening to some kind of music plugged into his ears and looked far, far away, as if he were not even there. Jonas appreciated this type of wordless moment; somehow he sensed that the youngster was sharing this moment with him in all trust. Jonas thanked God for inspiring him and told himself that he was resolute to help Stanley get back to a path where he could appreciate the fact that no man on Earth is never alone as long as he has God and the willingness to do good in his heart. We are all imperfect creatures, he thought, and we should never be too prompt to pass judgment on anyone. Instead, get the facts and try to understand the best you can. Jonas somehow knew that Stanley did not kill that man and that the truth would prevail.

Two days later the investigator came to see Jonas. Somehow he was not surprised. He wore the same rumpled suit that he had on the last time that Jonas had seen him and the same grim smile on his face. The man's appearance would definitely make one wonder if being a policeman was not the worst-paying job that existed. However, behind that unengaging demeanor, Jonas was convinced that there was a very astute mind. He did not fool Jonas one second.

- How are you today, Father?
- Fine. What can I do for you this time?

- Oh! You've already done plenty. You cannot imagine how restful it is when someone is doing this job for you.
- What exactly do you mean by that?
- Well, you brought the young man back here from his parent's farm. That made our job less prying. The youngster is no longer our prime suspect, but he remains a person of interest.
- I don't quite follow you.
- There have been new developments in Father Claude's murder. Apparently this priest of yours had several victims who wished him harm, in addition to all those allegations about his other activities we are now probing into. Your father was a busy man. We don't even know how he had time to pray to God.
- How could he have had so many other activities? His presence was well documented here with his daily duties, including the night masses. At least that I can vouch for.
- He had other means that we are unraveling right now. Unfortunately, this youngster was not the only victim he had here, but don't we all have favorites?
- If I understand you correctly, he had a thing for Stanley?
- You can say that again.
- Poor thing. What exactly do you want from him?

- We are drawing a profile of the deceased and talking to anyone we know was in intimate contact with him.
- But as you say, he is no longer a prime suspect.
- No. You see, whoever killed Father Claude did not leave any sign or clue that could have been picked up by our forensic team. This lack of evidence on the crime scene prompted us to look in another direction. Teenagers, no matter how smart they are, are creatures of habits and tend to leave their trail by being negligent, especially when it comes to what they wear, touch, and eat. They can do some awful things, even commit murder, out of spite or hatred. However, this particular case was just too clean. It did not fit the pattern.
- So where to now?
- Don't know yet. I'll have to speak to that young man. I promise you that whatever comes up I will keep you posted. I have a funny intuition that we have yet to unravel the true scope of Father Claude's activities.

The investigator turned out to be a very meticulous person who searched for the minute details, or lack thereof. Jonas knew that he would not volunteer all the information in the evolution of his search for the murderer of the priest, but Jonas had already gathered that Father Claude was no angel and that he did more than molest a number of the adolescents he had responsibility for. Jonas thought again that evil was never too far from good. He wished that God could tell him which path of the faith would be the easiest to comply with, since the challenges were everywhere on the road to redemption. How could a man who took an oath to serve and help his fellow men use it to cover the most heinous crime of all through deceit and abuse? Far from me, he thought, to say that this murder was a logical outcome of his misdeeds, but it takes true faith to pray for the salvation of such soul. Where would lie even the minutest glimpse of innocence when an adult can prey on children?

That evening Jonas lay awake in his bed, thinking of his mission and the challenges ahead. He thought that all men of the cloth should empower young adolescents because they represent the future and the melting pot from which the Church would find the next generation of priests. They were like good soil where the seeds of dedication to the service could be harvested in order to promote the goodness of charitable souls. The sacerdotal life was truly a life that necessitated a level of self-awareness in order to understand the mission. It was a fallacy to believe that a priest could find the validation of his calling through self-denial. That would be to confuse sacrifice with nihilism. How could anyone pretend to guide his fellow men when he did not know his true self? The strength and the resilience of a good priest rested in his capacity to transcend the many superficial aspects of ordinary life while respecting the established divine order of the universal path to higher levels of purification. He thought of the old man of his early days and his initiation journey to that fairyland of Pampuyo.

Was he that blessed? Or was all this consequential to an inspiration that brought him where he was, what he had become? He'd never really questioned his own evolution because his faith was apparently revealed to him without reluctance on his part, as if he were already prepared, resolute to accept God. He knew that it was not that easy for others, but God was here for everybody, and he believed that the simplicity of this truth made it so unreal.

Jonas finally rested that night, but not peacefully. In his sleep he saw himself fighting a horde of demons that invaded the school. The children were horrified, but he defended them with supernatural powers that he never knew he had. At the end of the confrontation he saw a bright light at the entrance of the school complex and the old man, who was smiling at him. When he finally woke up he found himself at the foot of his bed, holding his crucifix in his right hand. It was not over yet.

The boarding school was comfortable, and the youngsters received a highly rated foundation. During the school day they had practically no contact with the outside world but had plenty to keep their minds alert and productive. They met other children at school and sport events. They had the use of their computers, though many sites were blocked. Most of them had permission to use their cell phones, but only during their free time. These youngsters were being groomed to stay at the top of the social ladder. The transmission was done in a way that they did not see anything else. For them, it was the normal way of growing up. Jonas's duties included regular reviews of the curriculum and flow of the activities. He could not give information on the students, only when they were away visiting with their families and parents. Living in close quarters for so long during the academic year made the board of directors and the diocese very conscientious about how they were to mix studies, field trips, and recreation. Jonas thought that they had this well balanced.

As for Stanley, Jonas could say that the boy was as natural as ever. Being a sportsman, Stanley had many friends and participated in many extracurricular activities. However, Jonas had to admit that he always found an uncomplicated way to approach him and politely ask how he was doing.

The days went by, and Jonas had not heard from the investigator. Probably the questions he asked Stanley gave him sufficient information so he could carry his lump some other place! As for the community of priests living on that campus, there was nothing in particular to say about them except that they never ceased to express their mistrust toward Jonas, who was so used to that kind of treatment that he wondered if that did not baffle them. Well! Jonas had other things in his mind, things like when he would be allowed to leave this place and offer his services and his faith to a sector less materially fortunate than these youngsters. Probably because of his own upbringing, Jonas was never comfortable with lots of creature comforts; he was happy with the basic, necessary things to sustain his modest existence. Maybe that was one of the reasons that he chose to follow his calling for the priesthood. One could see it as a sin, but Jonas was growing weary of his current duties. He still felt that it was not his calling. On all accounts pride had nothing to do with the way he felt. It was just that being the prefect of discipline at Saint Peter of Compassion did not bring closure to what he felt were his real potentials. Nonetheless, he prayed and asked God for forgiveness if he in any way showed contempt instead of patience.

There was time to rejoice; Saint Peter of Compassion had been nominated as one of the best academic schools in the country. The announcement was well received by everybody. They were also good in sports, meaning that the attending youngsters were well taken of. Through all this, Stanley had not changed a bit. He was always the same courteous young man, weary from his studies. Observing him, one would never know the traumas he'd suffered from that deranged priest—or that was the way Jonas saw it. Things could not have stopped there, just like that. Sure enough, one morning the investigator came by his office.

- How are you, Father?
- Good. You seem preoccupied—having problems with the investigation?
- We are moving along. However, certain things are quite disturbing. I've spent a great deal of time in this job, but certain things I just can't relate to, like abusing and using young kids. I find this appalling.
- Evil has no discrimination.

- The further I advance in this case, the more dirt is coming up. How can a man lead such a double life right under the nose of such an elevated order, whose beacon remains the love of others?

- I gather that I should brace myself for disturbing new evidence.

- Yes. Father Claude was also dealing in drugs.

- Let's be clear—as a user or as a seller?

- We believe both. We did not pick any abnormality at St. Peter among the students, but a few priests are under investigation.

- Really?

- Yes, the delicacy of my mission is that I am walking on a tightrope under the watchful eyes of my superiors as well as yours, because they don't want any unnecessary scandals that could cause any additional lawsuits for the Church, which has its share of complications to deal with lately, in spite of how powerful and careful it is as the Holy Institution.

- You can say that again, but there are certain things that you just cannot avoid.

- I know.

- So tell me how I can be of help to you.

- I've gone through your personal file, and I found out that life was gloomy for you; you grew up in a very poor neighborhood. How from there you became a priest remains a mystery. However, by all accounts you have become a good and respected clergyman, in addition to your special training. I could not say the same for that deceased priest. Apparently he led a double life. We are trying to find out why he was murdered. As I told you before, based on his sexual deviation we thought that he was murdered by one of his students, but it turned out not to be so. Father Claude was murdered by an adult. The forensic evidence confirmed our theory, but our investigation will only be closed when we find out why, especially because of the drug aspect of his secret life. In any case, let's get to what brought me here today.

The investigator pulled a small object out of a plastic bag, and he said to Jonas.

- I'm taking a long shot, but we found this object among the victim's personal items and nobody could understand what exactly it is. We checked out your order, and this did not represent anything to them. I thought, based on your past, maybe you could help me understand what it is.

Jonas examined the object, and he felt a surge of embedded memories come alive in his mind. The object was a small talisman made of two strangely crossed axes with a sign of two half fingers pointing downward. It had been a long time since Jonas saw this emblem, but apparently not long enough. His past rushed right back in front of him.

- Yes, I know what it is. I am not glad to see this thing after all these years.
- What is it, Father? I need to know.
- I'm sure you do.

It took Jonas several seconds to steady his emotions while the investigator patiently waited. Jonas finally explained.

- You know that the entire city and its vicinity are divided into territories among the gangs that plague our everyday activities like termites in houses. To keep their business running correctly, many of them have developed signs and ways to identify them. It is not like in the movies. Most gangs operate according to several sets of rules that keep the peace among them and the flow of their business steady. All vendors are protected from one another as long their territory is well defined. Things break loose only when one of them steps out from his designated boundaries. Most of those who are roaming the streets carry an identification of some sort. This talisman happens to be just like one I was carrying when I was working for that gang on my street corner. If I felt that someone was paying too much attention to my activities, all I had to do was to pull my necklace out so they could see to whom I belonged and I was left alone. At least, that's the way it worked for me. How such an object ended up in Father Claude's personal effects is a mystery to me.

- Unless he also was working for the same organization as you once did.
- That would be farfetched—we don't even have the same background.
- It does not matter. What matters is how they infiltrated part of your God-fearing community and to what extent Claude was involved with them.
- The only way to find out is to touch base with the supplier.
- And that's where, Father Jonas, I need your help.
- I don't see how or why I should.
- Simply because we believe that some of these youngsters are part of this scheme, and the only possible way we see to block the extension of that web of devastation is if you would be willing to help us and your community.
- Do you imagine what I think you are trying to make me do? I'm not a choir boy, you know.
- I could not have chosen a better way to phrase our intentions.
- Let us say that I agreed. You know that I would have to be relieved of my duties here.
- Of course.
- How will I go about contacting you?
- I will. In the meantime, arrangements will have to be made

The investigator left Jonas deep in thought. The ways evil searched out any little crack to infiltrate itself made him wonder about the all-seeing eye of God—or had Almighty God seen so much of His own making that He at times was weary of us? Our imperfections, Jonas continued thinking, look more like a sharp plunge into the myriads of our mistakes instead of a special chart that measures our ups and downs. It is so easy to see God that it blinds most of us; just looking at a tree, a flower, or even our own body testifies to His Greatness. However, it was apparently easier to stick a needle in a vein to seek an artificial plateau of fulfillment that was only short-lived, never to be reached again. Jonas thought of this everlasting fight, knowing so well that at the end only Good could prevail.

THE MISSION

Jonas received his transfer papers to an inner-city Salesian parochial school not far from the place where he grew up and started selling dope. It was not a boarding school. Strangely enough, he never knew this school existed for all the time he'd spent around it. It was drastically different from Saint Peter of Compassion but nonetheless with the same basic curriculum. This time Jonas had no specific assignment, except that he was attached to the logistics department of the school, Jean-Bosco. The first thing that grabbed his attention was the dress code. Everybody was in uniform, with the school insignia and the student's full name on the shirt. The children looked the same to him, just slightly rougher. Stepping out of that complex, you knew automatically that you were in rough neighborhood. Jonas was not ashamed to notice how at ease he was roaming around familiar places, even though many years had passed since he was last there. He had been lucky, or was it simply his destiny? Jonas never really questioned in depth the path he took; somehow it looked normal to him, no more or less than a bit different.

What a turn of circumstance! Who would have thought that after leaving this place as Jonas, the small-time pusher, he would return after a few years as Father Jonas Victor? The passing of time had altered the old neighborhood for the worse; it had become more torn down, tawdrier, and surely more dangerous. Everything surrounding the institution was at the opposite of what was anchored in the minds of these needy kids by way of faith, education, discipline, and hope for future advancement. That was no easy task. After school hours the youngsters left school in small groups; it was safer for them to get home that way, since most of their parents were working far from where they lived. The young kids learned at a very early stage of life how to take responsibility, and anyone could see that on their faces. They delivered a special code of ethics into their surroundings. Surely they took pride in being different from the sprawling criminal enterprises synonymous with the area. They rose above. Needless to say, the motivation Jonas had to explore any avenue that could disrupt all evil efforts never ceased to present a picture-perfect image of his misdeeds.

Jonas did not dwell on establishing a plan for how he was to go about getting in touch with his old employer per se. He knew exactly how to go about things. Contrary to what many misinformed people might think, nothing was done in a hurry in the 'hood. With apparent disdain, everything was double-checked, just to make sure that someone was not some undercover agent looking for a quick score. Climbing the ladder of tolerance, not even trust, was always an uphill effort for the newcomers. First Jonas had to make his presence known, and the best way for him to do that was to go back to his old corner with his new identity. He knew what was expected of him. The Church did not like any unturned stone, especially when the sniffing around was done by another entity while one of its members was involved in shady activities that could in the end affect the Holy Establishment.

Jonas made himself very present in the community by visiting the needy and by participating in as many community activities as he could, but most of all he interacted with the crowd by playing basketball with them and bringing a few things, like cookies, new balls, and sports accessories. Slowly he started to gain status in their eyes. However, he insisted on going around his old corner because he knew that that would be questioned by the top guys, who made sure they knew everything that was going on their turf. The hazardous buildings, ruined pavements, and shadowy streetwalkers would never tell how much money was being manipulated there. The school was truly a beacon of hope in the midst of so much desolation. Even as an inspired educator, no one could come into these surroundings knowing that he or she would be able to magically improve the way of life of so many people, particularly young kids exposed to all kinds of loopholes that the Devil could sweep under their feet. Any group, organization, or congregation would know that it took many drops to fill a cup of accomplishments. But there could be no room for discouragement, because that what exactly what Evil was waiting for in order to gain ground wherever he could, particularly in such favorable settings. Jonas knew that he had to bring his unquestionable contribution by ignoring the immensity of the task but rather accepting the importance of any good deed, whatever dimension it could be. Armed with these positive thoughts he waited for his moment to come.

After a while Jonas was aware that every time he stepped foot outside he was being watched. One day he decided to go into a fast-food place nearby to have a hamburger with some iced tea. While he was leisurely treating himself, a young man approached the table and matter-of-factly sat beside him.

- Fancy seeing you here, Father. You've been walking around lately—do you miss your old turf?
- You seem to know a great deal about me, but I cannot say the same about you.
- You really look like someone who is looking for something.
- Probably souls like you, in order to see how I can bring the words of our Lord to you and your friends.
- Are you afraid that something might happen to you around here?
- As you already know, I am from around here. I still feel at home, just like you do, it seems.
- Different times—more dangerous.
- I can imagine, but tell me—do you have any plans for your future?

- Probably if I live past twenty-five, just like you.
- I remember that song. Do you know that the rapper who did that song made a name for himself? This is not the end of the world, you know. Look, not far from here we offer a good education to kids whose parents believe the future can hold better options for them if they allow their minds to see beyond these walls. God helps those kids to succeed.
- Easy for you to say. In any case, we want to know exactly want you want, wandering around like this.

Instead of answering, Jonas pulled out the talisman he was carrying and asked the young man if he recognized it. There was no word to describe the surprised look on his face when he asked Jonas if it belonged to him. When Jonas told him yes, he wanted to know everything about him. Jonas was somewhat disappointed that his talisman had more meaning than his being a clergyman. Finally he said that he assumed this was the point where Jonas would say, Take me to your leader. A big and mischievous smile appeared on his face. He told Jonas that he would have to report to the head of his gang; whenever he had something to tell him he would let him know. In the meantime Jonas would just have to go about his duties and walk around like a good priest. Since the streets were open for everybody, he was certain that he would find a way to contact him. Just like he came, the young man left.

Jonas took the time to take a good look at the man's appearance. Granted that he used to walk the street and manage his corner selling drugs not too long ago. However, the dress code surely had changed a great deal: saggy pants hanging below the buttocks, large T-shirts over tattooed arms, heavy metallic necklaces, and the strange hairdos said a lot. There was something despicably threatening about the young man's attitude and looks that made Jonas shiver at the thought of failed opportunities to save many young minds and lives. Had they failed out of disdain or ignorance, even though the Church had been around for a long time? Did they only look for the good few while pretending to have no fear of bringing the good words of the Lord to all mankind, no matter where they were and no matter how toxic a situation could become?

Upon returning to the Church grounds, Jonas remained deep in his thoughts. As a matter of fact, mankind is truly a social creature that needs constant supervising in order to function properly or according to the laws defined by his environment and calling. From any church or government, even to the worst gang, there has to be some type of hierarchy, from leaders all the way to the foot soldier. And when one looked at it, the pattern did not really change, except for who was first and who was last. And the struggle goes on and on in between...

Jonas could not show any sign of hurrying outside the church facility, because if there was one thing that he learned, it was that many people were being watched without even realizing it. And one thing was certain; he was resolved to get to the bottom of deceased Father Claude's activities. Time was on his side, although he did not know exactly what he was looking for. In the meantime he went dutifully about his responsibilities and took pleasure in seeing hope in the youngsters who looked so innocent and vulnerable. Jonas asked God to guide him even more so that he could accomplish as much he could during his lifetime. Deep inside him, he knew that evil would not prevail.

Jonas was growing weary of the cat-and-mouse game. He was aware that every time he stepped foot outside the seminary complex someone was there to follow his every move. He smiled at the thought that anyone who did not know better thought that these types of gangs were not organized and that they did everything, including shooting anyone, without careful thinking. Everything had to go at their own pace as perceived by them… Fortunately he had been very busy with a new program that they were trying to implement in the school. This program was very captivating and helped the students access easier means of learning the sciences and mathematics. Even Jonas got the hang of it, mesmerized by the things that the human mind could generate for the betterment of the species. This interlude was welcome in their everyday routine. But every time he had the opportunity, he went back to his old neighborhood, as if it were the most natural thing he could do with his free time.

One day, the same young man approached him at the fast food restaurant and told him that certain people would like to meet with him. Jonas said to himself that this was exactly what he was searching for. He agreed upon a day and a time without letting the kid see his enthusiasm about it. The only thing he did after was to inform those responsible for him being in this so-called effort to understand Father Claude's murder of the latest development in the situation.

Sure enough out of nowhere, the investigator was asking to see him.

- Why do I feel that I should not be surprised to see you are in a hurry to see me again since we last spoke?
- Well! Father, I still have an open investigation, and I hate to let my cases go cold.
- What can I do for you? Time is flying.
- Actually, nothing. I came here to give you a piece of advice.
- That being…?
- These kids are no angels. You should be very careful with what I feel you are about to do. You can get entangled in their web of lies and mischief, and it will be very difficult for me to protect you.
- I thought that my life was in the hands of our Lord.
- Nonetheless, just because you came from around here does not make you invulnerable to many situational shifts that can be detrimental to you and those you serve. Besides, I still have a vested interest in what you do.
- Am I in disturbing or slowing your work since we last spoke?
- On the contrary, but you are doing what I am suppose to do, if you know what I mean.

- Rest assured that I do, but you must also understand that we ought to shed a clear light on the death and murder of Father Claude too.
- For what direct purpose?
- Simply put, we are educators, and entrusted into our hands are many young lives to protect and nurture.
- In our separate ways we are here to serve and protect.
- I could not have said it better. What is your next course of action?
- My instincts tell me to let it flow with you. The department is looking for a murderer and a possible way to dismantle a gang that so far has been slick and hard to penetrate, whereas you are on a mission to unravel any connections that could affect the Church in any way and form. All I can tell you is that we will do our best to have your back, so at the end you will be able to tend your spiritual calling safe and sound.
- I want you to know that everywhere we go and whatever we do, we translate our deepest goal to reconcile the people with our God through the Eucharist.
- Amen, Father.

And he left without adding another word. Jonas reflected on the conversation he'd just had with the investigator, concluding that he was never too wrong when he left him under the impression that he was taking everything very seriously. Everything about the man made him seem more like a shadowy individual who could become dangerous if needed. He reminded Jonas of a character that he used to watch on television when he was a child. At the end Jonas decided to leave things as they were while awaiting the next episode in his quest for the truth.

Finally the day arrived when he was finally to meet with the young dealer's boss. He wasn't surprised it was the same house that he used to go once. The only surprising aspect of the meeting was that he met with the same guy he used to. He was slightly older but about the same generation, another proof that one could grow old in that illicit way of life if you knew how to watch your back. Apparently he was quite delighted to see Jonas; surely the same thought ran through his mind. He greeted him like the old acquaintance that he was.

- We finally meet again, after all these years. I see that you've changed your line of business.
- Well! I try to serve our Lord.
- Just like me. I help the needy, and I believe we are both doing well. As you can see, the streets have not yet had the last word on me.
- Probably because you don't use what you provide.
- You can say that again, Father. I see that you are back in the old neighborhood.
- I go where God sends me.
- I'm sure there must be some truth in what you are saying. We gathered that you are looking for some enlightenment that has nothing to do with your

mission as an educator—or have you become bored with your present duties on this Earth?

- Maybe both.

- In that case, Father, there is a good chance that you will scratch my back while I'm rubbing yours. We've wasted enough time sending smoke signals to each other—since we are old acquaintances, let's stop beating around the bushes. You are around here because you were conveniently transferred and also because of the tragic death of Father Claude. It happens that on all levels I'm glad to see you.

- I can't wait to hear why.

- First of all, we are aware of the gruesome murder of that man. And for starters, let me tell you we are also trying to figure out why he was killed.

- I still do not see how you can be related to him.

- Be patient. This may come as a shock to you, but the father was also working for us, and I dare say that he had a good and regular clientele. You see, we all are in the business of soothing the existence of our fellow men, of course from different angles, leaving the final appreciation to the receiver. His death came as a loss to us. We are not in the business of killing people; we report our activities more closely than any accountant does. So if anyone makes a mistake and ends up physically harmed, we don't want to know about it. If we accidently do, you won't hear it from us. This allows me to run a clean-cut business. What a sad loss! But fortunately

I believe we can make some type of arrangement with you.

- I don't see how. As in any other business, to repeat your word, you can lose some.

- I have an advantage over many others. Once you are hooked I become your savior. I am sure you of all people can truly appreciate the weight when people like us use the word *savior*.

- You are very intriguing. One day you should come to mass with me. Maybe that will help you better appreciate the difference between the two of us.

- I want you to pick up where Father Claude left off, as simple as that.

- How interesting! What makes you so certain that I will accept? You don't even know his clientele.

- If I don't know his clientele per se, as you put it, I damn well know how he made himself recognized to make his business worth his degrading vice.

- You are also informed about this sad aspect of your old dealer?

- Yes, just like I am aware of your ongoing collaboration with that detective. But what you do with him is not yet of a concern to me. I have plenty of time to get to him. What I want to finalize with you is how and why you will go on with my business.

The man is arrogant in many ways, Jonas thought, but I need to get to the bottom of this situation.

The Church had been embroiled in many scandals, and its hierarchy was quite aware of all the difficulties that rested on any priest's vocation to serve. However aggrieved they felt facing an ever-challenging world, they were all aware that this confrontation between Good and Evil was embedded in the subtleties of pursuing the goal to achieve what God had chosen them to do on this Earth. Unfortunately not all had the strength and perseverance to place any human temptation beneath the supreme value of their calling. Now Jonas was rubbing shoulders with an evil man who dared draw a comparison between his drug dealings and the mission Jonas so heartily accepted under the guidance of the old man after their mystical journey in timeless Pampuyo. Jonas always thought of his calling as a privilege that should never be overlooked or abused. He did not listen to that pusher with any condescension; on the contrary. While his ears were taking in this so-called enrollment, his soul was looking through, imploring God about how he could bring the light of God to this unfortunate social survivor, who would always blame the system for his past and present living conditions. Or was this pusher one the Devil advocated? Who knew for certain what his mission was?

Finally he told Jonas that he would get in touch with him again. He had certain arrangements that he had to make and outing him in front of a fait accompli. Jonas was determined to get to the bottom of this tragic affair, so he politely said yes to that clown, who probably thought that he held some divine power.

Here he was again, in the midst of a destiny that he was yet to define. As usual Jonas found healing through his prayers and his religion. So he waited for the day that creature would make his phone call to follow up on their last encounter: no pain, no gain. The effort to achieve a sensible clarity out of this mess had to follow this path, and that he knew. So Jonas waited. It was time for him to reassess his personal growth and count the blessings one could get out of serving sincerely and unequivocally.

The call came when he least expected it, but he was ready.

If it were not for the substance involved and the harm it was doing, anyone would describe their meeting as a routine business coordination. Jonas was to pick up where Father Claude had left. He was to receive by messenger a large box, in which was sealed merchandise, with the code name of the receiving party on each package. In order to let the clients know that he was the new delivery boy, Jonas was to wear the cross upside down on his left-hand pocket, with a red button below. The already designated clientele would approach him and give the name on the package, regardless of the real name, whether he knew it or not. All Jonas had to do was to deliver the packages and not worry about the circumstances before and after his task was accomplished. All this operation was well tuned; the right hand obviously did not actually know what the left was doing or who it belonged to. One thing for certain led Jonas to conclude that they definitely had no apparent interest in killing Father Claude. According to the contact he had done a good job.

Then who had reasons to eliminate the man, and what made it so difficult for the investigator to have an idea where to start looking?

Fortunately the dice started rolling very soon after the framework was put in place. Not once did Jonas have to exchange unnecessary words with any of his customers; he was just a "mail box" and accordingly could not see how he would advance in his search. The "customers" kept him busy. At first he was very nervous about doing this type of thing, but since apparently nobody gave a damn about his movements, he came to assume that everybody saw all this as within the normal realm of his duties within the community. However, what struck Jonas the most was the number of drug users among his own congregation, leading him to wonder how many priests were addicted to drugs and where they got the money to sustain their habits. Had the world gone mad? Jonas knew that he would never have the answers to all those questions, but just raising them put him in front of a harsh reality he defined as loneliness or maybe boredom, which was not an excuse.

And in that abyss, he wondered where and how would anyone pinpoint the sinful? Without blasphemy, Jonas was tempted to redefine what exactly a sin was. So many words were so lightly used in so many situations that in the end they lost their power on the soul. The irony of all of that justified his problematic quest to be an official soul caretaker. How challenging, he thought. The bottom line was to keep the entire spectrum as one entity of love. The mind could handle the intricacies of the job description by keeping matters as connected as possible. The rest would eventually depend on how things moved on. Inevitably, Jonas came to inquire how the Church could have survived all these centuries. Obviously the positives overwhelmed the negative aspects, and he was one of the unwilling witnesses: the Church prevails.

The days passed inadvertently quickly. One afternoon, out of the blue, the bishop came by with an inquisitive look on his face. He wanted to know if Jonas was pursuing Father Claude's murder and if he had been in touch with certain people of questionable reputation. Jonas told him that ever since his talk with the cardinal, he thought that it was his duty to try to clarify any subject that could antagonize the Church, and that was exactly what he'd done. The bishop insisted that he was not to put himself in harm's way just to straighten certain inconvenient circumstances. He reminded Jonas that the Church had had many centuries of practice and many moments of trial. The bishop's speech was an attempt to get to the focal point of Claude's misbehaviors, which had unleashed several unclear situations that were drug related. He emphasized that Father Claude's story was only one among many that the Church as a whole, under the guidance of the pope, was paying close attention to. In a word, the Church was undertaking a serious overhaul to cleanse itself after many misdeeds. He reminded Jonas to never forget that the Church was part of society and would always be imperfect. Finally he said that Cardinal Antonelli personally counted on Jonas's knowhow to bring this matter to the right conclusion, without direct Church involvement.

That brought a smile to Jonas's face, and he said that had always been the remedy over the last centuries: move softly and let time do the healing.

In a gesture of good faith, Jonas received a simple and sizable milk box containing all the unclaimed personal effects of Father Claude, with a simple note telling him that he hoped that would help him help them understand. With a glance, Jonas noticed that there were all kinds of personal effects in it. He put the box by his bed, promising himself that he would get into it after the evening service. When he finally retired to his room, Jonas started to go through the things in the box. Gradually the real Father Claude started revealing himself to him. As he unraveled the various items, Jonas progressively realized that the real Claude was not at all what he projected to his fellow clergymen. He'd led a twisted double life. According to his personal journal, he came from a single-parent family, and his mother had constantly molested him, although at the time he did not understand what they were doing. She had constantly told him that they came from a rare breed and that they had to keep to themselves for strength, protection, and comfort. Much later he found out that she had been raped and never said one thing to anybody. She kept her child. She was a very religious woman who went to church three times a week and participated in Bible classes on Sundays.

As Claude was growing up, he had problems reconciling their hidden activities with his own religious upbringing. He came to the conclusion that she was constantly battling some evil state of behavior and was unable to get rid of it.

She only found some type of closure through incestuous behavior with her son, while praying constantly to God for her final release. She died of a massive heart attack when he was only thirteen. The priest at the church where she used to go rescued and raised him, never knowing what kind of childhood he had. So Claude entered the priesthood, either for lack of knowing otherwise or in fear of the outside world. As an adult he always had a particular admiration for young children because of their smarts and their innocence. He could not recall exactly when he started having closer relations with them, but he knew that it came naturally to him, although he knew quite well that it was a sin. He never confided in anyone except another priest, who was about the same age as he and whose name was Vladimir. They always managed to find time for each other away from anyone else's sight and attention. They finally developed a physical attraction for each other and engaged in a very brutal sexual relationship while Claude continued "playing" with his selected pupils. From time to time Vladimir went along with his games and never said anything about it. Their pupils were so well-behaved and had good grades, and certain parents confided in them. This even allowed them to gain the trust of their superiors, who were so satisfied with their devotion that they went out of their way to have the two to teach and serve in the same schools for many years. Claude related to those times as the best years of his life.

One day he had to give a seminar in an inner city in preparation for the kids' first communion. Father Vladimir could not go with him because he was sick with a heavy cold, but he gave him a phone number and told Claude to pick up a box for him. That was the first time he met the pusher. It raised his curiosity, and he had no problem confronting Vladimir with his apprehensions. After a long deliberation, he agreed to go along with Vladimir, not because he was an addict and did not know it but because he needed the money to take care of a younger brother who developed a rare muscular disease in his adolescent years. Like Jonas, he had no family. Claude did not explain how Vladimir got into the business. However, in his journal he explained that Vladimir never fully recovered from the cold and finally died of it. Shortly after, they contacted him about taking over the job because so many of his fellow priests were behaving badly due to the lack of their substance. That was becoming worrisome. So the community included an alarming number of clerics walking around high on drugs.

If Jonas were to read in between the lines, he could imagine that part of Claude's hierarchy was quite aware of what was going on. Since there was no scandal, they just looked the other way while praying for the situation to end. Their prayer was not answered. The business went on and probably flourished to the point it finally had repercussions on the principals. Jonas did not find any pornographic or embarrassing materials in Claude's belongings except for a simple picture of Claude with Stanley taken on a field trip. Based on the picture's background and a note from Vladimir, they were demanding a great deal of discretion from him.

Since his eyes were getting the best of him and knowing that he had a long day ahead of him, Jonas decided to take up where he'd left off whenever time would allow. He was certain that the document and other items in that box would connect the dots. In the meantime he was puzzled by the expression of faith overlaying many questionable tendencies. The question lingered: where was the sincerity of their sacerdotal mission? Jonas was lost for words and thought over the meaning of his own presence within a world where he craved to understand its core sincerity while empowered by so many trustworthy followers. Was this his test, his personal challenge? The investigating side of Jonas's mind was looking for a link or an indication that could help him if not resolve at least understand why Father Claude was so brutally murdered.

The days came and went as if he was evolving in two separate worlds, completely estranged from one another. On the surface everything was normal, and nobody even mentioned the unfortunate incident. The drug users were subtly getting their doses and saying, "God bless you, Father" as if they were receiving communion. Jonas was so disgusted that he wondered how long he would be able to sustain the charade. However, at the same time he was beginning to clearly understand Claude's corrupt pattern. Jonas knew that there were people who sincerely were serving their fellow men, but this was beyond his worst nightmares. If he were to achieve his goal, the clerical community should ready itself for several nervous breakdowns or, even worse, priests taking their own lives due to their inability to obtain their regular substances. That would be a disaster Jonas was willing to confront for transparency and veracity of the faith.

Among several unimportant things in that box was another item that caught his attention: a carefully folded piece of paper. When he opened it, Jonas realized that it was a letter from Stanley. The letter was terribly menacing. He was telling Father Claude he believed that what existed between the two of them was a secret and a relationship that God wanted, just like Claude had told him. If Stanley had any doubt that Father Claude was doing the same thing with anyone else, he would make him suffer in a terrible way. The letter really made Jonas reconsider the circumstances involving Father Claude's murder and the conclusion that was previously reached. This turn of evidence could have a great deal of consequence for the archdiocese and the school, without naming the Church. If Jonas's suspicions had made a one-hundred-eighty-degree change, the eminent danger would be the investigator, not Stanley, as the main suspect. This information Jonas refused to keep to himself, because if at the end the moral responsibility were to come out, he surely did not want it to fall upon his shoulders as the one who'd obstructed justice for the image of the Church. He went straight to the bishop.

The man was not very enthusiastic to see him and hear of his apprehensions regarding the murder and Stanley. Jonas spoke, and the bishop surely listened before he told Jonas that what was done was done, and he'd better let the police do their work. Under no circumstances should he go around acting like a cop. He said he gave him Father Claude's box because he was certain that no matter what, Jonas would come to him first. Jonas proved him right, and now he was supposed to keep his mouth shut. So Father Vladimir died of natural causes and Father Claude was murdered. Stanley, meanwhile, was being the perfect rich youngster he'd left at his previous post; everything was closed and done with.

Jonas continued his routines with a great many unanswered questions, dutifully knowing that God's will in any matter always prevailed. Since he always was good in math and science, they sent him back to St. Peter on a temporary basis, since the priest in charge was involved in an accident and apparently it would take a while before he recovered fully. Within the congregation and even sometimes with outside help, they used substitute teachers in cases like this one. In this particular case, considering the geographical proximity of the two institutions, it was normal that they sent him instead of another from much farther away who was probably not as good. Jonas was excited about this temporary interlude for the direct duties regarding the children. On a much more personal basis, this would give him the opportunity to see Stanley again.

Although he had ulterior motives, he was glad to see the young man apparently in good health and high spirits. Stanley did not appear one bit disturbed to see Father Jonas again. On the contrary, he greeted him with a "welcome back, Father" that seemed very sincere. Jonas had too much on his mind to indiscriminately accept his greeting. Although resolute to have a talk with Stanley, Jonas felt it was premature to just jump on the young man and bombard him with questions that undoubtedly would leave him very suspicious of Jonas's ulterior motives. He wisely let it pass for the moment. Besides, he did not want to overlook the bishop's words of wisdom per se. Jonas had to admit the difference between the two institutions. Although the same quality of teaching was provided, if money talked it also made you do what you had to do in order to ensure its inexhaustible flow with a few elitist extras. It was obvious that the first was a school for the affluent, contrary to the one he was currently serving. Even the students had a different demeanor. Of course they did not do so on purpose; things were simply like that. It took Jonas a couple of days and some mental effort to backtrack to his previous position, so widely different were the two schools, but like the good teacher he was, that transitory back-shift went unnoticed. He was relieved. Some of the student cheerfully asked if he was back for good, unlike some faculty members. He told them that he was only there as a substitute teacher because the other father was sick. Nonetheless, they were glad to see him again. He actually enjoyed the classroom atmosphere. The kids were eager to advance their knowledge with a temporary new face. They wanted to impress Jonas, and that was very flattering to their regular teacher. Jonas considered the opportunity to teach as a blessing and could not fathom how any individual could take advantage of these young minds, so eager to excel. Unfortunately, the world was not an environment where all things were orderly organized. Looking at those youngsters, Jonas could not help thinking of the depth of his vocation and how elevating it was to be a part of the students becoming responsible adults. At the same time, he knew that he would fight with all he had any rotten, deviate mind that crossed his path, even if he had to use unorthodox ways for their own protection. This slippery walk that some of his colleagues took could not have other end results besides the many ways to expiate their misdeeds.

He finally crossed path with Stanley. Jonas jumped on the opportunity to engage him in a conversation.

-   How are you, Stanley?
-   Good, and you, Father?
-   Fine, except that I had an investigator from the police asking me all kind of questions regarding Father Claude's death.
-   I saw him around.
-   Did he speak to you?
-   Yes, but without insisting.
-   That's the way this man is. He always looks like his mind is in some other place. Stanley, I know that you were very close to Father Claude.
-   Just like many other kids, but at the end I grew to dislike him.
-   Why?
-   I did not trust him.
-   Was he that bad of a man?
-   Yes, he took advantage of me and others.
-   Why did you not report him to me?
-   It was too personal.

- I appreciate your sincerity with me, but do you think he should have been murdered that way?
- I don't know the details of his death.
- On the contrary, I'm sure that you do.
- And what difference would that make?
- To me, a great deal.
- Why is that he was not your friend?
- But remember that I had the responsibility to oversee everything.
- You are right.
- Since we have this moment alone, I can tell you that in his personal effects I found a letter that you wrote him a while ago, prior to his death.
- So there nothing to hide then.
- How can you be so detached about a man for whom you had such deep feelings?
- I knew that eventually I would have this conversation. I see that it took you a long time to get there. However, Father Jonas, let me tell you he deserved to die.
- Let us be straightforward. You don't regret that you killed him in such a gruesome way.
- How can you say something like that without proof?
- Stanley, I'm willing to hear your confession, because you need God's help to go on with your life carrying such a burden in your soul.
- You are confusing me. Do you think I had something to do with his death?
- Yes.

-   Then prove it.
-   No need to. My inquiries do not go beyond my duty as a shepherd of souls.
-   Father, I will come to confession when I feel the need to do so.
-   Very well.

Jonas had to admit that this young man was flawless, cool and collected. Sincere prayers brought to Jonas humility and modesty but by looking at Stanley he saw quite the contrary, and if guilty no sign of contrition. He dreaded the thought of describing him as a young cold-blooded murderer. Wisdom guided any apprehensions he might have had regarding Stanley's issues. He would have to wait and see.

In the meantime, Jonas went dutifully about fulfilling his role as a substitute teacher. The days came and went without any outstanding remarks, only the inquisitive looks of those with whom he could never get along, even when he was based at St. Peter. Apparently even the sight of him disturbed them, but Jonas had other things on his mind. He was thinking that by now the investigator should have let his presence be felt, but there was no sign of him lately. He'd probably concluded that the murder of Father Claude was a case that he would not resolve because they were such a tight community. Nonetheless, his prime suspect looked like the regular student he always appeared to be, nothing special or worth mentioning. So Jonas drifted through the days between his classes and his regular routines as a priest.

When the time came for him to go back to his post, he bid farewell to everybody and went as he came: silently. At that point there was nothing special to mention about Stanley; he was just about the same.

THE SNAP

It is not unusual that someone feels that his life has come to a standstill; everything seems to repeat itself with no hope of change. Jonas was having a dry spell. No day really differed from the one before. This was worse than boredom. He could not regroup his thoughts through prayers and reading. He was even questioning his true mission. Since his return to his post, things had not been the same; he was nervous and on edge. Something that he could not define was looming over his head that made him wonder what he could have possibly missed. He kept on reassessing Stanley's attitude, as if he were hiding something from the rest of the world. Or was Jonas having some type of premonition of things that had yet to happen? His alarming state of mind was beginning to affect him in many ways. One night he saw himself shaving a horned beast; he could not determine the kind or gender, but it looked dangerous. Another night he heard children crying in a den but was unable to find his way to them—they sounded so desperate and afraid! Once he saw himself in a dim light trying to find his way out of a strange house, but each time he got lost again. They say that anyone who believes in God has some type of superstition. Jonas did not take these nightmares lightly. He concluded that something was about to happen and that these things were just warnings preparing his state of mind, even though he could not foretell what exactly it would be. So Jonas went about his everyday life of service, prayers, and contemplation, waiting for what he concluded was inevitable.

On a cloudy afternoon, Jonas had just finished his last science class when one of the priests came into the room, telling him that he had to go to Father Superior immediately. When he got to his office he told him that there was a brawl at St. Peter, followed by a shooting in which Stanley was involved. There were three dead. When the police arrived at the scene of the crime, Stanley barricaded himself in a classroom, apparently heavily armed, and he'd told the police that he wanted to see Father Jonas immediately. Father Superior told him that he was not obligated to respond to that kind of request, and if he were to go he should tell the police. Jonas told him that he was going to see Stanley. Maybe that would prevent any further bloodshed.

On his way to St. Peter, Jonas could not help asking himself how this could have gotten so far and why he had been unable to pick up any disturbing signs from the boy. Jonas was very anxious to meet with Stanley. He prayed all the way, seeing no advantageous outcome to such terrible events. Fortunately, his education taught him that even when one was apparently at his lowest point, it never meant that the Devil had the last word. With help, he could find his way back to God Almighty.

Jonas felt that it took him forever to get to St. Peter. When he finally arrived on the scene, it looked like a battle zone: police cars, swat teams, and ambulances. All that could come out of Jonas's mouth was "Poor Stanley, what have you done?" He approached a policeman who appeared to be in charge and identified himself. The officer depicted Stanley as one of the most wanted criminals, and they were about to capture him, dead or alive. Jonas looked at him and simply asked for a megaphone. He identified himself and told Stanley that he was coming in. The policeman in charge wanted him to wear a bulletproof vest, but he declined. From the direction of Stanley's voice answering him, Jonas could tell that he was in a first-floor classroom that had a clear view of the front courtyard and entry and no direct access to the back. He had a very good vintage point. The entire place was empty, as he was well aware; that's how they knew how many people he had shot. When Jonas opened the door to the hallway, he saw two dead priests in a pool of blood. He did locate the third body at first.

Since Jonas knew the place quite well, it was not difficult for him to locate Stanley. When he opened the door of the classroom, he saw the third body. The blood was drier than the two others. He'd probably shot that one first. Stanley was in the art room, as expected, overlooking the front yard. Stanley had one rifle and two shotguns and plenty of ammunition. The scene was grotesque and macabre. It was horrifying to see a beloved student, a child, wrapped in such gruesome drama. It was logical that Jonas asked himself what had happened to turn this young adolescent into a murderous beast. So many questions were jolting through his mind that he had to make a serious effort to regain his composure. He walked in and just sat next to Stanley without saying one word. Through the crack of a window Stanley was observing the activities of the police. After a moment he fired a shot and obviously hit one of his assailants, because he said, as if talking to himself, "They really underestimate me." Jonas waited patiently until Stanley spoke to him, because he simply did not know where to even begin.

- We meet again, Father.
- Yes, but I wish that the circumstances were different.
- I know, but that's the way I want it. I asked for you because I wanted you to hear my last confession.
- Let's not be so definite.
- Hear me out anyway.
- Okay! But allow me to recite with you the best prayer that He taught us. If you don't want to say a word, He will still hear your voice.

When Jonas finished praying, he could feel that Stanley was less aggressive and better disposed to engage calmly in what he wanted to tell him.

- You see, I met Father Claude the first year I came here. I was a very insecure child and thought that my being born was a mistake. Claude took me under his wing and built my self-esteem. Unlike my parents, he made me feel worthy of being here and valuable to myself. Things, at least for me, started innocently. We were just playing. Anytime I told him that our playing used to leave me with a sense of emptiness, he always replied that it was probably because we were so enthusiastic, and he even added that he felt the same way. When I reached puberty, the physical sensations got more intense, and the outcome was always the same. At that time I did not know that I was just ejaculating. I could go into all the salacious details with you, but all you ought to know is that I grew fonder and more attached to the man. I truly thought that I was the only one and our "secret" was so special that nobody else could relate to it. As time passed on, I not only learned to know that it was an abnormality and child abuse—and quite common—but also that he was doing the same things with others. I had no place to hide and nobody to turn to.

- You could have come to me.
- You must be joking. To me, you were the personification of the perfect priest. You seemed to always be in prayers. You are cordial, but something in you makes people hope that they will never be misjudged by you. You should hear how we talk about you. While we think that the other priests are a result of circumstances, you seem to have been

born for what you are. Even your demeanor is always the same: very peaceful… the perfect priest. But at the end of my deception and with my resolution to end my life the way I see fit, you are the only person to whom I feel I could say, as a direct intermediary to God, Forgive me, Father, because I have sinned. You can imagine my disdain for Claude and myself.

- But killing other people beside Claude only made matters worse.

- Evidently! I wanted to get to a point where no human redemption could be available to me, so I made matters worse. Vultures like Claude should never be offered compassion or amnesty.

Stanley stopped talking. Just like that, he started by firing a shot at the police outside. He made sure to send Jonas at bay, a short distance between the two, while still being a much easier target. He knew that the police were maneuvering to get to Stanley and take him alive. But apparently this was exactly what he did not want to happen. Jonas could tell that Stanley was quite aware of the situation, and after what he'd done, there were not that many alternatives. Aside from the killings, he was punishing the entire establishment that had allowed a creature like Claude not only to find a tolerant circle that was appropriate for his predatory drives but also a community that always tended to do the utmost to protect its own reputation instead of protecting all the young victims, including himself. Stanley did not have to say a word for Jonas to assess the degree of his disappointment and the repulsive feeling he must have developed toward the institution.

Outside the police were progressing. Stanley sensed that he was running out of time, and that made him even more unpredictable and dangerous. All of a sudden the room was filled with choking smoke, and guns were shot. The last thing Jonas remembered, it was as if something exploded in his chest. Everything else went blank.

BACK TO PAMPUYO

Jonas really could not really tell what had happened. But he felt was as if it did not matter. This time, to get to Pampuyo he had to walk through a tunnel of incandescent lights that were bright but did not affect your eyes. On the contrary, the lights were like a shower that cleansed everything, including the surroundings. There was no way to describe the beautiful scenery. There was nothing in his mind capable of detailing what he was seeing. He was not aware that he was walking; it felt more like floating. To accent this harmony, soft music came from flutes that were hidden all over the place.

How did he get there? He could not remember, but he knew that his name was Jonas. Everything was blurry and foggy in spite of his efforts to make what he would say was the past tangible: nothing came through. However, he knew where he was. Could it be that he had a selective memory of the past? Because when an old man came to him, Jonas immediately remembered him as the one he'd already met.

- How are you, old man?
- Fine, as always.
- Why am I here again?
- You were an unfortunate victim of a gun fight. No need to get into the details. It was time for you to come back here because you have other things to do.
- Strange! I don't feel anything.
- It is simply that you are in another dimension where there is no need to have a material identity. You need to let your mind absorb many things. Above all I have to take you to a place unfamiliar to you from your first visit here.

Based on Jonas's own perceptions, they did not walk but floated. And they did not actually speak; it was better described as mental communication, nothing physical. The place was utterly beautiful, nature at its best. He turned to the old man and asked him where God was in the midst of this entire breathtaking atmosphere. He said that everything and everywhere he saw was Him.

This time the old man took him to a remote area of this wonderland, and much to his surprise Jonas saw an isolated place, truly uncommon to what he had previously seen. The closer they drew to the place, the more he noticed a repulsive odor coming out of the place, which looked like a big factory. When they finally arrived, Jonas came to understand that the creatures he saw were handling what smelled like human feces. They were feeding an endless conveyor belt. The stench was unbearable. At the end of that conveyor were several feeding machines into which the excrement was being poured and mixed with several other ingredients. The assembly lines were as long as the feeding process. Much to his surprise, at the end of that production process, all he saw coming out was money, jewels, precious metals and stones, anything that could induce covetousness—all the earthly objects that exemplified the dark side of human nature. It took him a while to let that scene sink into his brain. The old man looked at him and simply asked him if he understood. Jonas said yes. Basically, any human being has the duty to turn any situation or matter into good deeds. He also has to go above and beyond earthly attractions in order to reach the nirvana of wisdom through simplicity. The old man made sure to remind Jonas that it was not given to anyone to come to Pampuyo more than once. There were indeed several stages before one could reach the point of understanding: see no evil, do no evil.

Jonas was not sure how much time he spent in Pampuyo, but what he could attest to was that he saw the world in a different way. If man is a beautiful creature, he is by far the most refined of His creations. It is one thing to say, "Let us make man in our image and likeness," and another thing to really know how close the image is to the Supreme Being.

Since there was no evidence of the passing of time in the dimension where Jonas was, he simply could not assess how much time he'd stayed there. However, the longer he stayed the more he learned, and gradually his last moments with Stanley came to him. He had been shot, too, but Jonas did not encounter him in Pampuyo. Possibly one was sent according to how life had ended, but that no longer mattered to him. Strangely enough, Jonas knew that wherever he was, he was learning.

It had been a while since he'd last seen the old man, but he was not surprised to see him again. Of course he had not changed a bit. His appearance was still the same: calm and collected. Jonas never saw him laugh.

- It is not your fate to remain here while awaiting transit to a higher level. Your work is not yet done— you will have to go back.
- What can I say? I don't even know your evaluation methodology.
- In that case, just trust us.

Jonas had to admit that the trip back was not pleasant at all. He seemed to suffer all the hardships of men's misdeed while plunging into some type of darkness, totally the opposite of where he'd left. At the end he found himself seated on the same bench where he used to see the old man. Interestingly, the scene had not changed. He was watching a young man nearby, about his age, doing exactly what he used to do on that street corner: sell drugs. After a while the young man started looking at Jonas on that bench. Unable to restrain his annoyance, he walked toward Jonas.

- Why are you looking at me like that, old man?

And then Jonas understood.
It was the beginning.

ABOUT THE AUTHOR

Eddy Guerrier has worked more than thirty years in the insurance business, especially in his native Haiti. He graduated from Sheepshead Bay High School with honors and has a BA from Hamilton College in Clinton, New York. He is married, has children, and is a proud grandfather. Eddy enjoys reading, classical music, and traveling.

ABOUT THE BOOK

After selling drugs on a street corner, Jonas Victor opens his heart and finds God as the result of a series of circumstances . He witnessed how some men with the moral responsibility to elevate human souls let their twisted minds get the best of them. For Jonas, all these ways represent a path to God.